Robin Cannon received her BA and MS degrees from Fordham University in New York City and her Sixth Year Degree in Education Administration from Southern CT State University in New Haven, CT. She has been a schoolteacher for thirty-five years.

Robin lives with her husband, Bob, daughters, Haley and Molly, and son, Colin.

Three previous books written by the author entitled *Tilly Fig, Rye Hill,* and *Fireflies at Nightfall*—all published by Goose River Press—were displayed at the 2017 Book Expo in New York City. Austin Macauley published the fourth book by the author in 2018 entitled *The Vanity of Robbers.* Robin Cannon has been a guest speaker at Book Club meetings as well as the West Haven Public Library. She has attended book signings at various bookstores in Connecticut, including Bank Square Books in Mystic, Burgundy Books in Westbrook, R.J. Julia in Middletown, Warehouse Books in Clinton, and Barnes and Noble Bookstores in Westport, North Haven, and Milford. Additionally, Robin has interviewed with the New Haven Register, the West Haven Voice, and Hartford Books Examiner about her books.

PIGNOLI AND THE CHOCOLATE THIEF

Robin Cannon

AUSTIN MACAULEY PUBLISHERS™

LONDON • CAMBRIDGE • NEW YORK • SHARJAH

Copyright © Robin Cannon (2020)

Ordering Information:
Quantity sales: special discounts are available on quantity purchases by corporations, associations, and others. For details, contact the publisher at the address below.

Cannon, Robin
Pignoli and the Chocolate Thief

ISBN 9781643787367 (Paperback)
ISBN 9781643787374 (Hardback)
ISBN 9781645365013 (ePub e-book)

Library of Congress Control No: 2019919985

www.austinmacauley.com/us

First Published (2020)
Austin Macauley Publishers LLC
40 Wall Street, 28th Floor
New York, NY 10005
USA

mail-usa@austinmacauley.com
+1 (646) 5125767

For my children, and an adventurous little mouse they lovingly called...Pignoli.

I would like to thank my daughter, Haley, for showing me just how smart and fun pet rodents can be. I would also like to thank my sister, Holly, and my friend, Jeanine, for reading the first draft of this book. Finally, I would like to thank our mouse, Pignoli, for escaping from his cage for a three-day adventure before we could catch him and put him back...a much fatter and happier mouse. He was the inspiration for this book.

"There is nothing better than a friend, unless it is a friend with chocolate."

Charles Dickens

"Enjoy this chocolate-covered skittle skattle story...and the sweet recipe that follows right after it!"

Robin Cannon, Author

Chapter 1

Skittle-Skattle

Alas! There is no safe refuge for a mouse, even the smallest among them, far too small to carry a lima bean, or clench the tiny feather of a gold-crest in its teeth, or even climb the most diminutive of empty food cans for a morsel of nourishment. It is true! Life is full of hardship for these ever-scrambling squeakers who live out their days a smidgeon at a time.

Of course there is the obvious exception of Pignoli, a very resourceful and clever mouse. Always on a noble quest to escape the annoying limits of his tiny existence, Pignoli knew nothing of the welcome opportunity that was about to present itself until it did...a life-altering occurrence upon which he would quickly seize, thanks to his wits and an uncanny knack for sensing a good skittle-skattle adventure.

The Arancia train station, decidedly spectacular and the place Pignoli called home, was busy and bubbling with all kinds of folk who were either merrily going somewhere or dutifully returning from somewhere else.

The trains proudly whistling as they passed by were a wonder to Pignoli, who was now crouched in his favorite tiny corner watching in awe as he nibbled on a fallen crumb of some sort. Even the sitting trains were a sight to behold, although not as exciting as those that were slowly but surely clickety-clacking over the tracks.

Arancia was proud of its bustling and imposing train station, all that was impressive within this tiny village, for everything else was small and insignificant...the houses, the streets, and even most mice. Yes, that is what I said...*most* mice. For on this random yet fortuitous day, Pignoli would be given a rare chance that only one in possession of a clever nature would have recognized. An open carpetbag would mean nothing to a common or foolish mouse, the likes of which would never dare to dream as he did... this giant among mice.

Adept and quite sure of himself, for now we know that this mouse is no stranger to recognizing a good opportunity, Pignoli skittle-skattled across the crowded platform towards a tall, slender woman who was seemingly unaware that her carpetbag was wide open. This unintentional invitation caused Pignoli's heart to race, for it had been days, maybe even weeks, since he had experienced a real adventure.

It was true that he had narrowly escaped the clutches of a famished hawk only two days before and, yes, nearly three weeks ago he had gotten himself stuck to the platform for several minutes when he accidentally scampered over a discarded wad of chewing gum...a most silly situation! But those were not *real* adventures; they were merely two of the many trappings that can inconvenience a mouse over the course of a meager existence fraught with danger.

No...*this* was a *real* adventure, so on toward the carpetbag! Pignoli continued to skittle-skattle, dodging with an uncanny flair the long strides of the villagers rushing to board their waiting trains. Where they were going, he did not know.

When he reached his destination, Pignoli looked up to see a certain Signora Nonmaltobello, who was not a very nice person, screeching like an old crow. This he knew, for old crows had a foul screech...and her screech was quite foul.

"Ticket prices are far too high!" she screamed at the conductor standing by the waiting train, her shrill voice enough to make the hair on the back of his neck stand straight up.

"But Signora," the conductor countered, feeling a bit intimidated by her screech, "you are going all the way to Le Clerc!"

"A mere stone's throw away!" Signora Nonmaltobello blurted out in her screechy, scratchy, foul way as she waved a black umbrella in the conductor's face.

Pignoli listened to the exchange most carefully, as he sized up the length of Signora Nonmaltobello's long, black dress. He thought... and then thought some more. He knew what he had to do and now was the time! In a blink...a mouse's blink...Pignoli quickly jumped onto her dress and climbed his way through the many folds and creases, anxious all the while that his white, furry self would be spotted, or that the prickle of his tiny, sharp nails would be felt through the voluminous taffeta dress. He need not have worried.

Having scampered his way up to her hip, Pignoli knew that he was as close to the open bag as he would ever get. Holding his breath while tightly closing his little beady eyes, he leapt with all the strength he could muster, right into the blackness of the cavernous bag. Having gone completely undetected, he, too, would now be traveling to Le Clerc!

Pignoli knew that he must have landed himself onto a soft piece of clothing tucked inside the bag, for his arrival was quite pleasant, not to mention comfortable. Surprised and pleased at the same time, he snuggled into the soft cloth, proud of his bravery and, of course, his cleverness, for these were the very character traits that had landed him there in the first place!

After her exchange with the conductor, Signora Nonmaltobello snapped the carpetbag shut, plunging Pignoli into total darkness. Still nestled in the soft piece of clothing, he felt a bit queasy, as the bag suddenly moved to and fro. Signora Nonmaltobello was finally boarding her train.

"All aboard!" Pignoli could hear the conductor shouting as he rang a bell. "All aboard!"

Within a few short minutes, the train abruptly jolted as it proceeded to pull away from the Arancia train station...clickety-clack, clickety-clack.

"First stop...Montagne Nuageux!" shouted the conductor.

Pignoli settled back in the darkness of the carpetbag, folding his tiny hands as he placed them behind his head. He closed his eyes to take a much-needed nap, for he felt certain that he was bound for the adventure of a lifetime in that faraway place called Le Clerc. And indeed, dear reader...he was!

Chapter 2

Out of the Carpetbag
and into the Orphanage

The clickety-clack sound of the train over the tracks melted away as Pignoli fell into a restful slumber. He would dream about this adventure that he was on, this chance of a mouse's lifetime, fraught with danger and filled with excitement. Every minute of every day would be memorable and the people of the town of Le Clerc would know that a heroic mouse, fearless and true, had walked among them. Perhaps he would even meet a mouse to love, and dare he dream that she might actually...love him back? Knights in shining armor and damsels in distress flashed past in his tiny mind's eye...scenes of him gliding over rapid waterfalls... climbing up steep mountains...rescuing the unfortunates who had been waiting a long time...too long...for a mouse such as him. Pignoli wriggled within the soft cloth inside the cavernous blackness of the carpetbag, this dream of such adventures enough to make this snoozing mouse toss and turn in anticipation. It was the best dream that he had ever had in his entire skittle-skattle life.

Pignoli's pleasant dream would slowly subside, for the clickety-clack of the moving train jolted him awake once more. Suddenly slowing down, it came to a screeching halt as the carpetbag, the safest and most comfortable refuge he had ever known, jostled a bit in the seat beside Signora Nonmaltobello.

Pignoli thought that, perhaps, he should come up with a plan after all, for suppose she unexpectedly decided to open the carpetbag? Even though it was pitch black inside, he could tell by the touch of his tiny hands and feet that there were several objects in the bag that she might require at any given moment, such as her spectacles, coin purse, and...but before he could finish his thought, the bag was picked up off of the seat with a jerk.

Signora Nonmaltobello and Pignoli

"Le Clerc!" Pignoli could hear the conductor shout. "This is the end of the line! Everyone off at Le Clerc!"

The carpetbag began to swing to and fro once more. Pignoli pressed his tiny pink ear to the inside of the bag in an attempt to hear what was going on outside. There were many voices...loud voices, soft voices, and one foul screech which he had hoped he would never have to hear again once he jumped out of the bag, in much the same way he had jumped in, and got away.

"To the Ouble' Orphanage," Signora Nonmaltobello ordered, "and make it fast! They were expecting me an hour ago!"

"Ahh...bonjour, madam," Pignoli heard a man say. "You must be the new matron of the orphanage."

"Yes, yes," she said curtly, brushing the man off with an abrupt wave of her hand, "do not waste my time with your words! Just get me there! How far must we travel?"

"The Ouble' Orphanage is just outside of Le Clerc, madam," the man assured her. "I can get you there in ten minutes."

"Then get on with it," demanded Signora Nonmaltobello who was *not* a very nice person.

Pignoli was certain that they were now in a buggy, for he could hear the clippity-clop of the horse's hooves. And strangely enough, his twitchy little nose could detect the faint aroma of chocolate... right through the carpetbag.

The village of Le Clerc sounded busy, much busier than sleepy Arancia, as people shouted to one another in friendly voices to buy this or try that, but those happy voices soon faded into the distance. At least Pignoli knew where he was headed. He had never been to an orphanage before...not exactly the adventure he had in mind... but he would make the best of it. As soon as Signora Nonmaltobello opened her carpetbag, he would quickly jump out and get as far away from her as possible. Only then could his adventure truly begin. Of this he was certain...or so he thought.

Faithful to his word, the buggy driver got Signora Nonmaltobello and her concealed tag-along to the Ouble' Orphanage in just under ten minutes, having navigated the twists and turns in the road with an urgency most irregular, for he wanted to unload his rude passenger as quickly as possible.

"Here we are, madam," Pignoli could hear the driver say. He most certainly helped the matron down from the buggy because that is what buggy drivers were supposed to do, and he was surely the one who lifted the carpetbag off of the seat, and gently placed it on the ground at her feet, for it had been handled with such tender caution that the wretched Signora could not have possibly been the one to have moved it...not after the way she had jostled it about as she got on and off the train, swinging it to and fro the way she so recklessly did.

As he held out his hand and waited in vain for a tip, the buggy driver could only watch in disbelief as Signora Nonmaltobello picked up her carpetbag and unceremoniously marched herself into the large front hall of the Ouble' Orphanage without so much as a backward glance.

A group of forsaken little scamps would be the only ones to greet her, the same ones who had driven off the last matron. Immediately surrounding her, the frenzied orphans squealed and shrieked the way small children do when they are excited, but Signora Nonmaltobello would have none of it. Suddenly opening her carpetbag, she plunged her hand deep inside in the hopes of retrieving her whistle, the most important possession of any orphanage matron. *The sound of it could drive away the devil himself*, she would often claim. But instead of the whistle, and quite unexpectedly, she found her fingers wrapped around her furry stowaway. Without time to think, Pignoli wriggled out of her grasp, climbed over and around various items inside the carpetbag and jumped out, landing on the floor at her feet. Startled, Signora Nonmaltobello screamed and quickly dropped the bag as the orphans around her shrieked with laughter and delight at the sudden appearance of this little creature.

Pignoli scampered in every which direction as Signora Nonmaltobello blew her whistle. The orphans pursued him in a willy-nilly fashion, for the panicked mouse headed nowhere in particular until he heard an interesting conversation taking place in a nearby corner of the large front hall.

"Ahh...and here is the magic coin behind your ear," said the handsome orphan boy. "I told you it would be there!" he said with a wide grin as he placed it in the hand of a pretty girl about his age. "And what will you guess is under the red handkerchief?" asked the boy as he pulled a red cloth from his sleeve.

"I do not know or care to guess," the girl said somberly with a faraway look in her eye. It was obvious that she was distracted and quite sad, for she too was an orphan. But that was not all that made her sad.

"Oh, come now," said the boy. "Are you not the least bit curious?" Without waiting for an answer, he pulled a bouquet of colorful wildflowers from underneath the red handkerchief and handed it to the disinterested girl. "Voila!" he said with a happy grin. "Does that not make you happy?"

"*You* know what would make me happy...besides being able to leave this place," she said.

"Then you shall have it," the boy said decidedly, causing her sad face to suddenly light up, if only for a moment.

"How will you ever do that?" she asked. "We are merely poor orphans who are stuck here, unclaimed and unwanted."

The boy was ready to tell her that she was *not* unwanted, and that he would go to any lengths to obtain for her what she so eagerly desired but, alas, he would not get the chance, for at that very moment a little white mouse climbed up his pant leg.

The boy's eyes widened as the frightened Pignoli quickly crawled into his pocket, turned himself around, and cautiously poked his little head back out again.

"Please help me," implored the frazzled mouse. His adventure had most certainly begun!

Chapter 3

You Shall Have It

The handsome orphan boy suddenly found himself in the midst of the disheveled little orphans who had been chasing Pignoli, the lot of them now quite astonished as the scampering white mouse had simply disappeared. Having understood Pignoli's plea for help, an unbelievable but true happenstance, the boy calmly pushed the tiny rodent deep into his pocket away from prying eyes. Gently stroking his white fur with one finger, he quieted his fellow orphans as Pignoli stayed perfectly still deep within the pocket, enjoying the soothing attention he had longed for his entire life. With his tiny pink ears, he listened gleefully, for it sounded as though he had finally found...a friend.

"Now, now kittens," the boy said with a calming voice, "what is all of this excitement about?" He smiled as he patted each of them on the head.

"The mouse! The mouse! Did you see it?" the orphans squealed as they jumped up and down, clinging to the older boy on all sides. Pignoli could feel their push and pull, for the boy had lost his footing more than once, this jostling him around the pocket as well.

"Easy now, my little friends," he said softly, putting a finger to his lips to quiet the excited orphans. "There *is* no mouse."

"Oh, but there is, there is!" they shouted.

"Well, if there *was* a mouse it has long gone, probably deep within a hole in the wall by now," he concluded, smiling and winking at the pretty orphan girl who had been watching the unfolding fiasco with her usual sadness. Even the boisterous merrymaking of the younger orphans could not make her smile, for the one thing she wanted most of all...was out of her reach.

Groaning with disappointment, the orphans hung their heads and dispersed, walking away in several different directions before Signora Nonmaltobello could catch up to them.

"You shall return to your rooms immediately and await my inspection!" she screeched in her most foul manner, blowing her whistle for good measure. "That includes the two of *you*," she barked at the handsome magician and his sad friend, who began to walk to their rooms, obeying the order of the new matron although in no hurry and decidedly unafraid.

"Remember," the boy whispered to her as they walked, "you shall have it...what it is that makes you happy." She smiled her sad smile in appreciation, but dared not even hope that he could ever get his hands on what she desired.

Giving her a wink, the boy walked toward his room, whistling as he went. *You shall have it,* he thought. As she walked toward her own room, however, the heart of the sad orphan girl was as heavy as ever, her friend's magic tricks and promises simply not enough to give her hope. *I shall never have it,* she sadly determined.

Having been unimpressed by the new matron, for they had seen so many come and go before her, both orphans closed the doors to their respective rooms, captives of their own thoughts as they awaited inspection, hardly giving Signora Nonmaltobello a second thought.

*****

As soon as he closed his door, the boy quickly reached into his pocket and gently removed a smiling Pignoli, who, by this time, was simply giddy with excitement for he had safely, although barely, escaped from the carpetbag of Signora Nonmaltobello.

Having moved on to a new phase in his improbable adventure, the tiny white squeaker was ready for anything, clapping his little hands in anticipation as he stood on top of the boy's small trunk filled with magic tricks, the only possession he had in the world which he guarded with his life.

"Well, what shall we do next?" asked Pignoli, his small, slender tail swishing behind him. The boy's eyes widened like saucers, for no mouse had ever spoken to him before.

"So you *can* talk," said the boy in amazement. "I thought I was hearing things."

"Oh no," said the mouse as he eagerly shook his head. "You were *not* hearing things. And thank you...for letting me hide in your pocket."

"You are welcome, my friend," said the boy as he smiled at Pignoli. *Friend,* Pignoli thought. *He called me friend.* "Aren't you a funny little fellow," the handsome orphan beamed as he gently

16

tickled the mouse's belly. "How is it that you find yourself in the Ouble' Orphanage?"

"I came from Arancia…by train…in Signora Nonmaltobello's carpetbag," said the tiny mouse. "The ride was comfortable enough, but I am glad to be out of her bag. She is most foul, you know."

"All the way from Arancia, you say? My, my, I *am* impressed. And who is this Signora Nonmaltobello of whom you speak so…hmm… fondly?" the boy asked, tongue in cheek, of course.

"She is your new matron, a most foul woman," Pignoli repeated as if it were a dire warning.

"Most foul indeed!" the boy laughed lightheartedly. "Well, well, so that loud woman with the whistle is Signora Nonmaltobello, the new matron from Arancia," he mused out loud while scratching his chin and smiling, if only slightly. "An interesting choice for a matron."

"Are you not worried? Are you not scared?" Pignoli asked breathlessly.

"Of course not," said the boy, furrowing his brow. "No matron has *ever* scared me." He *was* older than the other orphans, much closer to his majority as was his sad friend, and he *had* dealt with the likes of this new matron before…many a time. "By the way, do you have a name, little fellow?"

"I am Pignoli, formerly of Arancia, now of the Ouble' Orphanage just outside of Le Clerc," the tiny mouse said proudly, as he stuck out his chest. "And you? Do you have a name?"

"My name is Hammett," the boy giggled. "I think I shall keep you, Pignoli, for your presence here tickles me. Perhaps I can use you in a magic trick or two."

"I was never good at entertaining people," warned the mouse, waving the idea off with his tiny hands. "No one has ever clapped for *me*."

"Oh, do not worry about *that*," Hammett assured the mouse. "I am the entertainer around here. Just your simple assistance in one of my magic tricks could very well bring momentary happiness to my sad friend…until I am able to get my hands on what would *really* make her happy, that is," he said. But the boy had doubts.

"Tsk, tsk," he clicked softly through his handsome white teeth. "That will be a nearly impossible task, but I must get it for her sake. I promised!" He bowed his head and feverishly paced the room, searching deep within himself for the perfect plan.

"Does this friend of yours have a name too?" asked Pignoli.

"Of course," said Hammett. "*Everyone* has a name and hers is Trista."

"Well, what is it that would really make your Trista girl happy?" asked the curious mouse. "Perhaps I can help."

"Oh, I doubt that, my friend," said Hammett, stopping to give Pignoli a gentle tickle on the belly in appreciation. "Thank you for your kind offer, but what Trista wants will not be easy to get. You see, she wants..."

Suddenly, the foul screech of Signora Nonmaltobello could be heard as she made her way up the dimly lit hallway, inspecting the rooms of the dreary orphanage one by one. Pignoli jumped up in fright, but without hesitation Hammett quickly snatched him off of the small trunk filled with magic tricks and gently stuffed him back into his pants pocket. Barely had Pignoli had the chance to turn himself around and get comfortable, before Signora Nonmaltobello rudely intruded without so much as a knock on the door.

Hammett was charming, for that is how he normally behaved toward everyone, and the not-so-nice matron would not be an exception.

"Good day, dear lady," said the boy as he slightly bowed before Signora Nonmaltobello. At that very moment he could feel Pignoli squirm inside of his pocket. "My name is Hammett."

"Silence!" screeched the foul matron. "I do not care *what* your name is, as long as you behave yourself while I am here at the Ouble' Orphanage. You are older than the others," she quickly stated. "I suppose no one would have you." Such a shame...you are not a bad looking boy," she hissed in a low voice. "Nevertheless, I expect your complete cooperation at all times," commanded the matron as Pignoli, cradled deep inside of Hammett's pocket, winced at the sound of her voice.

"Of course, dear Matron," replied Hammett, bowing once again before Signora Nonmaltobello who squinted at the boy skeptically.

"What is in the trunk?" she asked abruptly.

"Oh, that is filled with my magnificent magic tricks," Hammett answered proudly. "Whenever I can bring pleasure..."

"Open the trunk now," the matron demanded, rudely interrupting the boy. Hammett complied, breaking his own rule to never reveal to *anyone*, not even a crotchety matron, what was inside the small trunk.

Signora Nonmaltobello looked inside, determined to poke around.

As she bent over, Hammett gently warned her.

"I would not do that if I were you, dear lady," he whispered.

"And why not?" the matron snapped.

"Because the last person to reach into my trunk lost a finger," the boy responded, grinning his boyish grin.

"Who was that?" Signora Nonmaltobello demanded to know.

"The last matron," Hammett confided.

"Impertinence!" the foul matron screeched as she backed up, this allowing the boy to instinctively close the trunk and change the subject.

"The sky in Le Clerc is lovely today, surpassed only by your own beauty, dear lady. Would you not agree?" he said, cleverly flattering her. Pignoli rolled over twice in Hammett's pocket, cringing with every fawning word he heard the boy say.

Not knowing what to make of the orphan boy, Signora Nonmaltobello was both flustered and perplexed, causing her to finally take her leave, but not before spitting forth an indignant remark, her bony finger raised high in the air.

"Magic is the devil's trickery!" she declared loudly. Hammett had to make an effort not to giggle. Then pointing her finger at him, she came up ever so close to his face and revealed her most foul self. "It is of little wonder that no one ever wanted you," she growled. "Just stay out of my way." And with that, Signora Nonmaltobello...was gone.

As Hammett wiped the matron's spittle off of his face with a handkerchief, Pignoli climbed out of his pocket and hopped back onto the trunk.

"I had hoped to be rid of her after jumping out of her carpetbag," he commented somberly.

"Do not worry, my friend," Hammett assured the mouse. "Stick with me and I shall protect you from Signora Nonmaltobello who is *not* a very nice person." Pignoli's heart fluttered because no one had ever offered to *protect* him before.

"Then I shall stay," declared the mouse, "for your proposal is as sweet as the faint aroma of chocolate in the village of Le Clerc!"

Hammett's eyes suddenly widened with surprise and his mouth fell wide open too, for his new friend had just given him a gift, a most wonderful and unexpected gift, far greater than any gift he had ever received.

"What did you say, Pignoli...about chocolate?" asked the boy.

"Le Clerc...smelled it," said the mouse that was now dancing a jig on top of the small trunk filled with magic tricks, entirely giddy with happiness over Hammett's offer to protect him. Finally, he had achieved his dream of adventure...and belonging. As for Hammett, he just smiled broadly as he watched his little friend, for he was now certain that he could make his Trista happy after all with the help of a tiny...white...mouse.

Chapter 4

A Mouse to Love

"Pignoli, my little friend!" shouted Hammett. "You are amazing...a genius! How did you know?" the orphan boy gushed, as he picked up the tiny white mouse and covered him with kisses.

"It just...came to me?" Pignoli said haltingly, for he was not at all sure of what he had done or said to deserve such praise.

"You and I will do great things together," said Hammett excitedly as he gently placed Pignoli back on top of the small trunk filled with magic tricks, "and our first order of business will be to obtain the very thing...the only thing...that will finally make my Trista happy."

"I am confused," said Pignoli, making a face as he licked his tiny hands and washed behind his ears. "I thought you told me that I could not help you with..."

"Yes, yes," Hammett interrupted, waving off Pignoli's remark with his hand, "but that was before I knew! What you have just said has changed my mind!"

"Knew what? And what did I just say?" asked the befuddled mouse.

"Chocolate...you smelled the faint aroma of chocolate in the village of Le Clerc!" shouted Hammett, delighted at the sound of Pignoli's words.

"So what?" challenged the mouse, still confused. "Why is that such cause for excitement?" Pignoli lifted his back leg and scratched the top of his head between his tiny pink ears. Perhaps he would better understand the reason for Hammett's unbridled joy if he were to knock some sense or, rather, scratch some sense into his wee brain.

"Do you not yet realize?" Hammett moaned, although with a smile from ear-to-ear.

"I cannot say that I do," Pignoli whispered sadly, as he wrinkled his pink twitchy nose feeling...well...quite foolish.

"Now see here," began Hammett, "if you and I are to do great things together then..."

At that moment, Pignoli's beady little eyes pooled with tears, for the boy seemed angry with him. How sad it would be to lose his only friend, and so soon after having just met him! When Hammett realized just how upset the tiny mouse was, he stopped what he was saying and decided to simply *tell* him what he needed to know.

"The only thing that will make my Trista happy is chocolate," Hammett began patiently, "and you claimed to have smelled just that, if only faintly, in the village of Le Clerc. That means that somewhere in the village there is a *chocolaterie* and you, my friend, will help me find it. Only then will I be able to get my hands on some chocolate and make my Trista…"

"Happy!" Pignoli shouted with glee, finishing Hammett's sentence for he finally understood! Just one thing bothered him, though. How could they possibly…pull it off?

"We must come up with a plan…tonight," Hammett insisted.

"Alright," said Pignoli, scratching his head once more. "I suppose we can come up with a plan. After all, the village is only a ten-minute horse and buggy ride from here."

"Where on earth would an orphan boy and his mouse find a horse and buggy to take them into the village? No…we shall have to be more clever than that," said Hammett, clearly weighing several options in his head as he paced the floor in silence.

"What could be more clever than a horse and buggy?" asked Pignoli, not understanding Hammett's reluctance to his suggestion. "It is not only fast, but it is classy too."

"Would you please forget about the horse and buggy," Hammett pleaded. "We must find a way to get to the village, find the chocolate, and then get back to the orphanage…all without getting caught."

"How will we get into the *chocolaterie*…or pay for the chocolate?" Pignoli asked in a bit of a panic.

"Do not fret, my little friend," said Hammett, patting Pignoli gently on the head with one finger. "Leave it to me. I will come up with a sure-fire plan after dinner. My Trista will finally be happy…just as I promised."

"Oh my," sighed the mouse, scratching his chin with his left foot. "I have managed to live this long and I do *not* want to find myself under the wrong end of a broom with a truffle in my mouth. I have not yet even met a mouse of my own to love…you know, the way you love your Trista."

Hammett giggled while Pignoli's twitchy pink nose and tiny pink ears flushed bright red with embarrassment.

"I will keep that in mind," said Hammett, still giggling. "You know, you are a funny, little fellow, and I am glad to know you." The orphan boy gently picked up the mouse and kissed him on the head before placing him in his shirt pocket. "Stay perfectly still in there, for it is time for dinner. Perhaps I can slip you a crust of bread or some such thing."

"I *am* starving," said Pignoli, "but can you not do better than a mere crust of bread? Why at the Arancia train station, I once found a discarded piece of beef smothered in brown gravy. It was delicious," said the mouse as he licked his lips.

"This is the Ouble' Orphanage, my friend," Hammett said softly into his pocket. "I can promise you a crust here or a crumb there, but beyond that..." Hammett wrinkled his nose. "I have not had a piece of beef myself since I got here over five years ago." The orphan boy suddenly had a faraway look in his eye and Pignoli felt sorry for him...and rightfully so.

That night, dinner consisted only of clear broth and a chunk of rye bread. Even without a horse and buggy, the idea of sneaking into the village for chocolate suddenly seemed inviting to the famished mouse.

*****

After dinner, as he stood on top of the small trunk filled with magic tricks, Pignoli nibbled on a rye seed while Hammett hatched his plan.

"We shall walk there...at night...under the cloak of darkness," declared the orphan boy with one finger in the air for emphasis. Pignoli swallowed hard.

"At night? In the dark?" he gulped. "How will we ever find our way in the dark?" The mouse had clear misgivings.

"I will take a lantern from the potting shed out back!" said Hammett, confident that his plan was coming together nicely, although he could see the grave concern on Pignoli's face. "Do not worry, my little friend. You will be safe inside my pocket the entire time except, of course, when we get into the village where I will need your twitchy little nose to sniff out the location of the *chocolaterie*." Realizing the importance, actually the necessity, of his role in the caper, Pignoli was understandably nervous...and a bit frightened.

"Suppose I can no longer smell the chocolate?" asked the mouse.

"But you *will* smell it," said Hammett. "You *must*."

The boy lifted the fretting mouse off of the small trunk of magic tricks after he had swallowed the last of his rye seed, and gently placed him on the hard, flat pillow of his bed. In an attempt to cheer Pignoli and take his mind off the plan for now, Hammett opened the trunk and carefully took out several of his favorite tricks that were sure to lighten the heart of the worried mouse.

There were the interlocking rings, the disappearing francs, and the Eiffel Tower card trick, all illusions that Hammett had mastered and enjoyed performing, especially in front of Trista. But alas, Pignoli could only sigh as he watched the orphan boy's magic show, for he was distracted by the thought of chocolate hunting at night in unfamiliar surroundings. To him this was dangerous and unnecessary. A daytime trip into the village was much more desirable to the hesitant mouse and must surely be possible...mustn't it?

"Do you not like my tricks, Pignoli?" Hammett asked, unsure of what else he might do to cheer the heart of the tiny mouse.

"I suppose they are fine tricks," Pignoli sighed, his mind clearly elsewhere. Suddenly, Hammett had a thought.

"If you come along with me to the village and help me find chocolate for my Trista, then I promise I will find something for you," said Hammett.

"And what might that be?" Pignoli asked sleepily.

"A mouse for you to love!" the boy declared. Pignoli sat motionless as though struck by a bolt of lightning. He then stood up and puffed out his chest, for his dream was coming true!

"Which night do we leave for the village?" he asked bravely.

"Is tomorrow night soon enough?" Hammett asked heartily while patting the mouse's head.

"The sooner, the better," said Pignoli decisively. It was time to meet a mouse...to love!

Chapter 5

A Sure Place to Find Crumbs

Pignoli slept well that night, between two lumps on Hammett's pillow. As the orphan boy snored, the tiny mouse dreamed, just as he had in Signora Nonmaltobello's carpetbag, of finding a mouse of his own to love, one that would actually love him back. With Hammett's help, he would certainly find the mouse of his dreams. And he was having such sweet dreams until...

Bang! Bang! Hammett sprang out of bed as though he had bounced off a trampoline, swiping Pignoli from his pillow and stuffing him into his nightshirt pocket without his usual gentleness.

"Stay perfectly still, little fellow," the orphan boy whispered, for having been through this so many times before, he knew exactly what was about to happen. Suddenly, the door to his room flew open, causing Pignoli to cringe at the familiar screech that pierced the air, the boy's pocket offering little refuge from the awful sound.

"Stand up straight," snapped Signora Nonmaltobello. "Be dressed and ready for breakfast in ten minutes! Your job today will be to wash all of the windows in the main hall, and then to scrub that filthy floor in the dining room!" Pignoli stayed perfectly still, just as Hammett had instructed. His excitement over breakfast *and* the filthy dining room floor, a sure place to find crumbs, must never show through a rippling shudder or, what is worse...a random squeak.

"My dear matron," Hammett began in a most mannerly fashion, "it was my hope that today I might pull the weeds from the garden. I promise to do an excellent job of it." With a final touch of charm, he smiled.

Smart, Pignoli thought. *That would give him access to the potter's shed...and the lanterns!* But alas, Hammett's savoir-faire came to naught.

"You shall do as you are told!" screeched Signora Nonmaltobello. "The weeds in the garden are of no consequence to me, for I do not care if they turn it into a jungle, but I shall not have foggy windows and sticky floors!"

Pignoli's excitement turned to fright as he trembled in Hammett's pocket, prompting the orphan boy to cover it with his hand.

"And make sure that filthy nightshirt is scrubbed clean today! It is crawling with...something!" the unkind matron bellowed, scowling at Hammett before leaving the room as though he were too repugnant to look at.

Pignoli slowly poked his twitchy little nose out of the concealed pocket just as Hammett lowered his hand, relieved that the matron was gone.

"You are safe, my friend," said Hammett, coaxing the tiny white mouse out of his nightshirt. "Let us go and have our breakfast now."

"But how will we ever be able to make our way to the potter's shed," asked Pignoli, "if you have to wash windows and scrub floors?"

"I will figure out a way," said the orphan boy. "For now, just prepare yourself for soupy mush." Pignoli made a face. He never thought he could miss the trash can at the Arancia train station so much, even though Hammett promised to give him whatever crumbs he could find on the dining room floor before scrubbing it clean. Life at the Ouble' Orphanage was certainly not the romanticized adventure he had dreamed of in the matron's carpetbag, at least...not yet.

Pignoli was still licking his lips when Hammett began to sweep up the dining room floor after breakfast.

"A distinctly milky taste," said the mouse, commenting on the soupy mush. "Not bad."

"Not good either," said the boy as he stooped over to pick up a blue button for possible use in his magic act, a dusty slice of carrot, and a dried kernel of corn from a meal that had been served over three days ago. He blew the dust off of the carrot and gently polished the dried kernel of corn on his shirt, before quickly stuffing all three items into his pocket.

"Do not eat *that*," Hammett whispered, for Pignoli had grabbed the pretty blue button first. "You may eat the carrot and the corn. They are good for you." The mouse made a face.

"I am not a vegetarian," he grimaced, "but I suppose they will have to do."

"You are a picky little fellow, Pignoli." Hammett smiled broadly. "Perhaps *this* will please you," he said after finding a stale morsel of French-fried potato on the floor.

"Now, this is what I call a treat," said the mouse, hungrily munching on the hard bit of potato. Perhaps this place was not so bad after all.

Hammett continued to sweep the dining room floor until he had a large pile of unrecognizable scraps mixed with dust. He then got on his hands and knees and scrubbed the floor clean with hot soapy water, causing Pignoli to hang on for dear life within the confines of his pocket for fear of tumbling out!

"I am perilously tipped, Master Hammett," warned the mouse in a frightened whisper.

"Silly little fellow," the boy said under his breath, "just hang on tightly." And so Pignoli did just that, for Hammett could feel the mouse's sharp little nails dig in through the cloth of his shirt. It was now time to wash all the windows in the main hall of the orphanage, and the timing was…perfect.

As Hammett entered the main hall, he could see that several of the floor to ceiling windowpanes had been removed by two handymen, making it possible to simply *step* out of the room and onto the grass behind the orphanage…if one chose to do so.

Of particular interest to him was the fact that *in* doing so, one might easily gain access to the potter's shed, a convenient hop, skip, and a jump out of any one of those windows.

While carefully sizing up the situation, he picked up a rag and the bucket of soapy water left for him and began to wash the remaining glass windowpanes in the main hall until the two handymen, who were apparently replacing rotting wood, decided to take their mid-morning break. Without hesitating the boy made his move, stepping out of one of the large, open windows onto the grass behind the orphanage. Running straight for the potter's shed he never looked back, but became suddenly worried that the shed door might be locked. It was certainly too late to turn back now!

"Hey!" cried Pignoli, bouncing up and down in Hammett's top pocket. "What is going on?" Without answering the mouse, for time was of the essence, Hammett ran up to the door of the shed, lifted the latch, and pulled. Voila! The door was unlocked. Leaving it open to allow the light to stream in, he quickly scanned the shelves of the dimly lit shed and grabbed the first lantern he spotted. "Hey!" Pignoli shouted again. "Why is it so dark in here? Where are we?"

"Be patient, my friend," said the boy. "Be patient."

Hammett ran out of the potter's shed, clutching the lantern with one hand while holding his shirt pocket with the other to keep Pignoli from uncontrollably bouncing about. Reaching the orphanage, he quickly stepped back through the open window into the main hall, but as fate would have it he bumped right into Signora Nonmaltobello...who had been standing there...waiting. Even without her foul screech, Pignoli could sense her presence, causing him to lie perfectly still within the safety of Hammett's pocket.

"Oh, dear Matron, how lucky it is that I have run into you," said the fast-thinking orphan boy, clutching the lantern in plain sight. "The two handymen, who are now on a break, asked me to retrieve this lantern for them from the potter's shed and I did so gladly," he said, setting it down by their toolbox, "but..."

"So why is it so lucky that you have run into me?" growled Signora Nonmaltobello, interrupting the boy while staring at him through two suspicious slits as her eyes had quickly narrowed.

"Well, there is nothing more for me to do in the main hall until the glass panes have been returned to their rightful frames, so I was hoping that you would, perhaps, give me another assignment." Hammett spoke with a charming twinkle in his eye. "Before you do that, though...please allow me," he said, reaching up and pulling the blue button that he had found on the dining room floor from behind her ear. Signora Nonmaltobello, however, was not impressed.

"Do not *ever* leave your job without *my* permission," screeched the matron in her most foul manner as she walked away from Hammett to examine the glass-free window frames. "Humph...tsk...tsk. Why was I not aware of the removal of these windowpanes? I will most certainly have a little chat with the handymen," she scowled, talking more so to herself than to the orphan boy. As she grumbled, Hammett kept a close eye on the lantern that he had placed near the handymen's toolbox.

"So, you took in a little breath of fresh air for yourself without my knowing," continued Signora Nonmaltobello, this time hissing directly at Hammett who was now cautiously backing up.

"I did not mean..." began the boy who was suddenly interrupted by a scream. Signora Nonmaltobello jumped, but only slightly with fright, for it would take something quite horrific to *really* frighten her, as she watched one of the orphanage nursemaids run into the main hall.

"*Petit souris, petit souris...juste couru a travers mes pieds!*" the maid cried out, a little mouse having just run across her feet.

Oh no! Hammett thought, quickly placing his hand over his shirt pocket. Indeed...Pignoli was gone.

"What! Again?" Signora Nonmaltobello screeched. "My broom!

My broom!" she shouted as she and the nursemaid ran out, leaving Hammett to stand alone in the middle of the main hall. The boy did not know what to do. Should he remain there? Should he run? Where oh where was his little friend?

No longer able to hear the vile matron's foul screeches or screams, for she was probably in a faraway room still searching for her broom, Hammett decided to inch his way toward the lantern. Getting closer and closer to his prize he began to sweat, for what would he do, or say to her, if she should suddenly return to the main hall? Clearly, Signora Nonmaltobello did not like him, even if he *did* pull a blue button from behind her ear. But the boy swiftly decided to brush his fears aside, for he had come this far and surely it would be pointless to remain frozen to his spot. Trista would never get her chocolate if he did so!

Still hearing nothing, Hammett looked around the main hall one last time before taking two lively steps that placed him directly next to the lantern. Swiftly grabbing it, he immediately stuffed it underneath his shirt and without further hesitation made his way toward the door of the main hall. Looking up and down the dark corridor that would eventually lead to his room he began to walk briskly, hoping that he would not meet anyone on the way. How fortunate it was for him that Signora Nonmaltobello had simply...disappeared!

Suddenly, and to his absolute delight, Hammett heard a voice...a squeaky, high-pitched, tiny little voice. Could it be?

"Wait for me! Wait for me!" the voice loudly cried out. Hammett abruptly stopped and spun around, relieved to see his adventurous little friend scrambling up the hallway after him...skittle-skattle, skittle-skattle. He quickly put his hand to the floor, enabling Pignoli to hop on. Stuffing him into his shirt pocket, he hurried toward his room, for he hadn't a moment to lose.

Reaching his destination without incident, Hammett quickly entered the drab room and closed the door quietly before falling onto the hard bed. His heart pounded excitedly while Pignoli breathed hard too, evidenced in the boy's shirt pocket going up and down, up and down.

"What were you thinking?" Hammett asked the mouse breathlessly. "Why would you ever leave the safety of my pocket? You could have been killed!"

"When Signora Nonmaltobello walked away from you to inspect the open windows, I jumped out of your pocket," Pignoli said proudly, still inside of Hammett's pocket.

"Whatever for?" the boy asked.

"To take her attention away from you!" exclaimed the mouse. "That way, you could escape with the lantern while she was chasing after me!"

"Hmm...a diversion tactic," Hammett commented, scratching his chin.

"Exactly!" shouted Pignoli, his little head now sticking out of the boy's top pocket.

"Dangerous...dangerous," Hammett whispered under his breath while shaking his head from side to side.

"It worked, did it not?" asked the mouse.

"Sure, but..." began the boy until Pignoli interrupted.

"Look, do you want the chocolate or not?" asked the annoyed mouse.

"You know I do...more than anything," Hammett said emphatically, "but I do not want you to get *broomed* on my account."

"The sooner you get the chocolate, the sooner I get a mouse of my own to love...you promised," the tiny mouse reminded his friend. This caused Hammett to pause, if only for a quick moment.

"All right, my little friend," he chuckled. "I *always* keep my promises, so let us get some rest, for tonight after darkness falls, we shall go to the village by lantern-light in search of chocolate...and a mouse to love!"

"What about Signora Nonmaltobello?" Pignoli asked nonchalantly as he, once again, snuggled deep down within Hammett's pocket.

"She will have to find her *own* mouse to love," laughed the boy. The tired mouse rolled his eyes. And the two friends giggled and giggled...until they fell fast asleep.

Chapter 6

An Odor Here...A Fragrance There

Both Hammett and Pignoli had fallen into a long, hard sleep... the kind where one barely moves other than to breathe, and dreams go unrecalled. But they would both be harshly awakened by the youngest of the orphans, whose job it was to walk the gloomy, dark corridors of the Ouble' Orphanage every evening with a bell that would summon the children to dinner.

"L'heure du diner! L'heure du diner!" shouted the spirited little boy with each clank of the big brass bell that weighed heavy in his small hand.

Hammett slowly moved his legs over the edge of the bed and sat up, yawning widely while rubbing the sleep from his eyes.

"What time is it?" asked Pignoli, his tiny head barely peeking out of Hammett's shirt pocket.

"It is dinner time," confirmed the tired boy, his answer barely audible as he struggled to shake off the haze of his deep sleep. Pignoli yawned too...a large, drawn out yawn that would have been the envy of other tiny mice, had they seen it.

"I am so tired," said the mouse, stretching his tiny arms, "but I am hungry too. That stale French-fried potato did not stick to my ribs the way I thought it would."

"Then let us be off!" Hammett proclaimed, suddenly feeling chipper. "Tonight we will need all of our strength to go into the village and find the chocolate."

"And once we have found the chocolate?" said Pignoli, one tiny reminder finger in the air.

"Yes, yes...we shall then find you a mouse to love, little fellow. I promise," confirmed the orphan boy, "but at this very moment, all I can think about is telling my Trista at dinner tonight that she will finally get her wish."

Hammett quickly grabbed his favorite magic trick out of the small trunk for good measure...the disappearing face trick, made possible only by his expertise in sleight of hand...and happily left his room. He looked forward to telling Trista all about the plan...in a whisper, of course.

"Remain perfectly still within my pocket," he quietly reminded Pignoli, but as they entered the dining room, the boy was stopped immediately by a foul screech.

"Stay right where you are!" screamed Signora Nonmaltobello. "Did you think that I had forgotten about you?" she asked, briskly walking up to him from behind. Hammett stopped in his tracks and slowly turned around. Pignoli remained still within the boy's pocket as instructed, but what he really wanted to do was jump out and bite the nasty matron right on the nose.

"Ah, my dear matron, I am so happy to see you again," said Hammett with a smile. "I waited for you in the main hall this morning for quite some time, but you never returned so I left, frantic over your well-being." Signora Nonmaltobello stared at the orphan boy for what seemed a long while as though she were considering whether or not to take him seriously, but as usual...she would have none of it.

"Children who leave the confines of the orphanage without my permission are not *allowed* to eat dinner, so you can just turn yourself around and go straight back to your room," the matron said sternly.

"But Matron, it was the handymen who beseeched my help. I was just tending to their need out of respect, for they are adults and I am merely a..." Hammett spoke politely, only to be interrupted.

"Back to your room," Signora Nonmaltobello screeched, "without another word!" The boy could feel Pignoli twitch slightly within his pocket as the tiny mouse thought of going to sleep that night on an empty stomach, but what was worse was the look on Trista's face as he left the dining room. Now, he could no longer tell her of his plan at dinner, but perhaps by tomorrow, he would have a fine chocolate truffle to bestow upon her, making all things right and good...making Trista happy.

Hammett returned to his room more determined than ever. He decided that at the stroke of nine, (he adored the number nine, for it followed the number eight with such dignity and was considered a lucky number in the world of magic) he would sneak out of the orphanage and make his way to the village of Le Clerc by lantern light.

"Once we arrive in the village, you will use your nose to help me find the *chocolaterie*," he reminded his tiny little friend.

"I hope my nose works without food in my belly," Pignoli said anxiously as he rubbed his stomach.

"When we find the *chocolaterie* you shall then have plenty to eat!" Hammett giggled. "We both shall!"

"I still say that we cannot just break into a *chocolaterie*," the doubtful mouse said seriously, climbing out of Hammett's shirt pocket and onto the small trunk of magic tricks.

"We will find a way in without breaking *anything*," said the boy confidently. "Besides, I thought that mice were good at getting into places, especially forbidden places such as kitchens, pantries...and *chocolateries*."

Hammett giggled again, for despite being thrown out of the orphanage dining room he was in a good mood. By this time tomorrow night, Trista would be so pleased. He checked the lantern to make sure it worked properly while Pignoli washed his face carefully with both hands. After all, if the boy *were* to find him a mouse to love, then how could she ever love him back if his face were dirty? Soon it would be nighttime and the sky would cloak everything in darkness, the perfect cover for an orphan boy and his mouse about to embark upon a forbidden journey.

That cloak of darkness fell quickly as Hammett changed his shoes from the ones with the hole in the toe to the leather hand-me-downs he liked to wear whenever the local abbe' visited the orphanage, bringing with him couples who were interested in adopting a child. So far, the shoes had brought him no luck, but tonight they would at least make his journey into the village a little more comfortable.

As he sat on the edge of the bed tightening the worn-out laces, there came a sudden knock at the door. Hadn't Signora Nonmaltobello screeched at him enough for one day? He sheepishly opened the door, prepared to charm the matron once again, but he need not have concerned himself.

"Trista!" Hammett called out with surprise, quickly pulling the sad girl into his room and closing the door. "I am so glad to see you, but what are you doing here?"

"I thought you might be hungry," she said, pulling a rather large piece of bread from her sleeve, "you and your little friend...if you still have him." With that, Pignoli poked his twitchy pink nose out of the boy's shirt pocket for, yes, he was still there and quite hungry indeed!

"As you can see, I *do* still have him," laughed the boy, immediately giving the nosey mouse a small piece of crust on which to nibble. "Now, do not make crumbs," he ordered, gently pushing Pignoli back into his pocket.

"I must go," said Trista.

"Wait!" Hammett implored, biting off a good-sized chunk of bread. "Please allow me to tell you what the mouse and I plan to do for you...tonight." The expression on Trista's face softened as the boy chewed hungrily while he explained his plan. "So you see," he said, "you *shall* have that which makes you happy." Trista suddenly became shy and lowered her eyes.

"Merci', Hammett," she said softly, her mouth turned slightly upward in a rare demure smile.

"You are welcome," said the orphan boy bashfully, for the two had never been alone before. His heart was pounding and he was afraid that Trista might hear it.

"I must get back to my room before the matron's bed check," she said quietly. "Be careful, Hammett." And with that, Trista quickly left the room, but not before giving the boy an unexpected peck on the cheek.

"You are blushing," said Pignoli as he climbed out of Hammett's top pocket and sat on his shoulder, licking the breadcrumbs from his tiny little fingers. "Hello? Are you there?" the mouse asked the boy, who had a faraway love-struck expression on his face. Snapping his fingers, Pignoli was able to break the spell that had overcome his friend...if only barely.

"Yes, I will be careful," Hammett finally mumbled, long after Trista had left the room.

"Oh *brother*," said Pignoli as he rolled his eyes. He quickly skittle-skattled over to the small trunk of magic tricks and climbed up to the top, his favorite place to sit, while Hammett regained his senses.

"Now we wait for the stroke of nine, my friend," said the smitten orphan boy with a new resolve before gently reaching up...and touching his cheek.

*****

At the exact stroke of nine, Hammett slowly tiptoed out of his room with Pignoli safely tucked into his top pocket. He carefully held the lantern with his right hand while clutching several matchsticks with his left.

"Move over," he whispered to Pignoli as he shoved the matchsticks into his pocket alongside the mouse.

"You are *squishing* me," grumbled the aggravated squeaker.

"Shhh! Keep quiet!" Hammett said in a loud whisper. "I *must* be allowed to concentrate, otherwise we will get caught!"

"You were lucky not to have gotten caught during the bed check," Pignoli scolded, "having been completely dressed, shoes and all...really!"

"All right, so perhaps I was careless, but at least I was completely under the covers, was I not?" countered the orphan boy.

"You *barely* made it," the mouse reminded him. "I think Signora Nonmaltobello knew you were up to something, for she stared at you through the darkness of the room for a good long while, looking for a reason to...pounce. Oh, how I *dislike* that word," winced the little fellow. "It reminds me of an alley cat I once knew."

"Let us forget about all that," Hammett said somewhat impatiently, although Pignoli's reprimand was duly noted. "From here on in we will pay attention to every little detail. There is so much at stake...for the both of us! You want a mouse of your own to love, and I want my Trista to be happy. It is no small task, what you and I are about to undertake, so please...shhh!" Pignoli hunkered down, once again, deep within the boy's pocket and closed his eyes, for it was his bedtime anyway.

"Wake me when we get to the village," he yawned. "You will not need my nose until then."

"That is an excellent idea," said Hammett who was a little anxious, now that the plan was actually underway. He patted Pignoli on the head with one finger as he crept through the darkness of the main hall towards the front door of the Ouble' Orphanage. "Pleasant dreams, little fellow. Pleasant dreams."

Just as Hammett expected, the usual nursemaid was stationed by the front door to the orphanage, sound asleep and snoring. A rather broad woman, she could keep a *flock* of orphans from leaving if she had been awake, but it was quite obvious that she valued her sleep and would not arouse easily. Relying on that, the orphan boy carefully removed the clapper from the bell above her head, allowing him to open the door without making a sound. After one last momentary hesitation he dashed into the darkness, streaking through the night air toward the village of Le Clerc, lighting the lantern only when he had successfully fled the confines of the orphanage, although Trista was never far from his mind.

The road to Le Clerc had its twists and turns, but Hammett could easily see them by lantern-light and before he knew it, the village lay before him. Stopping to catch his breath, he stuck a finger in his pocket and nudged Pignoli.

"We are here, my friend," he whispered to his tiny passenger. "We are in the village of Le Clerc!"

Pignoli tossed and turned inside of Hammett's pocket, but eventually stood up to stretch his tiny arms and legs while, at the same time, poking his head out to have a look see.

"Yes, this *is* the village, by golly," yawned the tired mouse.

"Well?" said Hammett impatiently.

"Well what?" Pignoli answered.

"Well, do you smell chocolate yet?" asked the boy anxiously.

"Of course not!" declared the mouse, rather annoyed. "I just woke up! Everyone knows that a mouse needs time to get his bearings before he can smell *anything*!"

"Nonsense!" Hammett replied, eager to get the job done, although he did wait for Pignoli to fully come to his senses. He had no other choice.

"Walk further into the village," the mouse finally ordered. "The *chocolaterie* is probably down the road and to the right."

"Are you sure?" asked Hammett.

"Well...hmm...not quite," the mouse stammered, "but my nose is beginning to twitch!"

"What does that mean?" asked the boy.

"It means that I am ready to sniff out the *chocolaterie*! Onward!" shouted Pignoli as though he were a knight on a noble quest.

Although dark, the lantern-light was enough to make it obvious to Hammett that the village of Le Clerc was a pretty place. There were several gardens and a fountain in the center of the village square, as well as the many carts and stands from which people sold their goods, now all covered over for the night with blankets. Pignoli's nose began to twitch.

"Lift the blanket on *that* cart, Hammett," the mouse directed, pointing to the one nearest the fountain.

"Do you smell chocolate?" the boy asked hopefully.

"No, but I smell cheese," said Pignoli, licking his lips while wringing his tiny hands. Hammett walked over to the cart at which the mouse pointed with the utmost caution, his lantern lighting the way through the eerie shadows. Afraid that someone might be looking at him, his eyes darted in every direction but, alas, there was not a soul in sight, for all of the villagers were fast asleep. He slowly lifted one corner of the blanket and sure enough, there were tiny crumbles of bleu cheese that had been left behind in one corner of the cart. "Put me down! Put me down!" Pignoli ordered. The orphan boy quickly obliged with a giggle.

"There you go, my little friend," Hammett said with a smile, "but be quick about it." And quick he was indeed, unable to recall having had such a treat in ages.

As Pignoli swallowed the last tiny crumb of cheese, his nose began to twitch again. Pointing to the cart on the other side of the fountain, he directed the boy to pick him up.

"Do you smell chocolate *now*?" asked Hammett, hoping for the answer he wanted to hear.

"No, but I smell green peppers," said the mouse, once again licking his lips.

"We are not here for cheese, or peppers, or..." the exasperated boy started to say before being interrupted by the blunt words of his tiny friend.

"Do you want to find the chocolate or not?" asked Pignoli.

"Of course I do," said Hammett.

"All right then. There is a process you know," said the mouse.

"A what?" the boy asked, his face now twisted in confusion.

"A process!" Pignoli repeated. "An odor of cheese here, a fragrance of pastries there, and a smell of vegetables across the way are all a part of the process!"

"What do you mean?" asked Hammett.

"Each aroma leads to the next...then to the next...then to the next... until finally you have arrived at the smell for which you have been searching! A *process*! Everyone knows about it!" declared Pignoli, sticking out his proud mouse-chest.

Speechless, Hammett could only nod, for it was far easier to agree with a mouse than to disagree. After all, he needed Pignoli's twitchy little nose to sniff out the chocolate, whether he liked the process...or not.

So, on to the cart in which green peppers must have sat during the day, for that was a part of the process. And as it turned out, much to Hammett's delight, Pignoli's twitchy little nose had been correct, for there in the cart remained two small green peppers. *Could the process actually be real?* The boy began to wonder.

Pignoli proceeded to nibble to his heart's content until his little pink nose twitched once more, signaling Hammett to pick him up and bring him somewhere else...to another cart for bits of apple... to a garden for scraps of bread thrown to the birds...to a lamp post under which an entire ladle of bean soup had been spilled onto the cobblestones...until finally, one last twitch of Pignoli's little nose would lead to...

"Down this cobblestone path!" declared the overstuffed mouse, holding his roly-poly belly with one hand while pointing the way with the other.

"What now?" the boy asked. "A whiff of roasted beef...a fragrance of cookies and cream? Pignoli hiccupped before he could answer.

"My dear Hammett," burped the mouse while lying on his back in the palm of the orphan boy's hand, "the process is now complete and I am too full to say...anything...further." And with that, Pignoli yawned, closed his eyes, and fell fast asleep.

"Pignoli? Little fellow?" Hammett whispered as he gently stroked the head of the tiny white mouse. "Do not fall asleep on me now... please...Pignoli." But the orphan boy could not rouse the little squeaker, for he was already dreaming of a mouse to love.

Hammett sighed a long lonely sigh as he stood in the dim light of the village square, Pignoli steadily snoring in the palm of his hand. Looking down the cobblestone path in despair, he saw nothing but darkness. He lifted his lantern and slowly followed the narrow path anyway, expecting to find nothing and, indeed, he had made his way to the very end without seeing...or smelling...*anything*. He hung his head as he turned around and began to find his way back, the unevenness of the bumpy cobblestones making the walk unpleasant, when suddenly Pignoli woke up, his nose twitching once again.

"Stop right here," said the mouse, sitting up in the boy's hand.

"Why?" asked Hammett curiously, relieved nonetheless that his friend had awakened. "There is nothing here."

"Oh, but there is," said Pignoli. "Go down that alleyway." Hammett lifted the lantern a little higher to see an alley off to his left. This, too, was quite dark. "Go ahead," encouraged the mouse.

"Are you sure?" asked Hammett.

"Quite sure," said Pignoli, still full and drowsy. The orphan boy obediently turned to his left and walked only ten feet down the dark alley before striking his head on a low-hanging sign that he had not seen, for the flame of the lantern had shrunk considerably.

"Ouch!" shouted Hammett, his cry echoing down the alleyway as he rubbed his head. "That hurt!"

"Voila, as you would say!" declared the stuffed mouse, pointing to the sign. Still rubbing his head, the boy looked up, lifting the dimly lit lantern to take a better look at the low-hanging piece of wood. As he read it, his eyes widened.

"Well, well...you were right, my clever little friend," Hammett whispered, still staring at the sign. "You were absolutely right."

He stood there, shaking his head in amazement. "How in the world did you do it?" Pignoli, of course, could only smile for he *knew* the answer to the question, along with every other mouse that had ever used...the process!

Chapter 7

To Catch a Thief

It was a beautiful sign...the most beautiful sign that Hammett had ever seen, and it simply read:

Chocolaterie Ledoux

Armand et Tumelo Ledoux

Propriétaires

"Well, I must hand it to you, my friend," Hammett had to finally admit, "this process of yours *really* works. I did not believe you at first, but I certainly believe you now."

"Oh, ye of little faith," cracked Pignoli nonchalantly as he yawned the biggest of mouse yawns, the trip into the village having exhausted him so. "A mouse's process *never* fails."

"I can see that now, little fellow, but will your process get us into the *chocolaterie* too?" asked the boy. "This door is locked," he confirmed after carefully turning the knob on the wooden door underneath the sign.

"Hmm," the mouse pondered carefully as he scratched his chin. "I am sure that there is a back side to this building. Let us walk down the alley a little further."

"What good would *that* do?" asked Hammett. "Even if we *can* get behind the building, it does not mean that we will be able to get inside." The boy was beginning to face the fact that a locked door was no easy hurdle.

"Will you trust me, Hammett? I just have a feeling," said Pignoli, "that you *will* have your chocolate."

The boy did not have the heart to tell the mouse that they had probably reached a dead end, and that their only hope might be to wait for the *chocolaterie* to open in the morning and simply *beg* for the chocolate. Of course, that would present a whole new problem... how to get back to the Ouble' Orphanage in broad daylight without getting caught by Signora Nonmaltobello. Could he be overthinking it? The mouse seemed to have no reservations at all and was getting decidedly...impatient. "What are you waiting for? Onward!" Pignoli ordered his friend, pointing a finger skyward.

So, onward they went...down the alley, then to the left, then to the left again, around several garbage cans, and over a tall mound of wooden crates until finally...

"Stop!" shouted the tiny white mouse, standing tall in the palm of Hammett's hand. He had obviously taken command of the situation. "We are here!" His tiny pink nose twitched from side to side, high up in the air.

"How do you know?" asked Hammett. Pignoli pointed upward to an open transom.

"*That* is how I know," said the mouse. "The *chocolaterie* is right inside of that window. I can smell it...the truffles, the bonbons..." But before the tiny mouse could finish his list, the boy had gently stuffed him into his shirt pocket and made his move. Quickly stacking a number of wooden crates, one on top of the other, he climbed up to the open transom and tried to squeeze through but, alas, he was simply too big.

"I cannot get through," Hammett said, his voice straining as he tried to cram his body through the small opening. Carefully backing out of the transom, he stood perfectly still upon the tippity-top crate and wondered what to do next. Pignoli, who had gotten somewhat squished during the effort, poked his tiny head out of Hammett's shirt pocket and, once again, gave the boy an order.

"Drop *me* inside of the transom and then wait in front of the *chocolaterie*," he instructed.

"Wait for what?" asked Hammett.

"For me to unlock the door, of course," said Pignoli, slightly offended. The boy knew better than to argue with an offended mouse, so he did *exactly* what the little squeaker had ordered him to do. Ever so gently, and against his better judgment, he dropped Pignoli inside of the transom, hoping that he would not have a long way to fall.

Frightened for the brave mouse, Hammett quickly jumped off of the stack of wooden crates and ran back...over the remaining crates, around the several garbage cans, to the right, then to the right again, and up the dark alley until he found himself standing in front of the *chocolaterie* once more, right by the wooden sign. It was there that he would wait...and wait...and wait...for what seemed an eternity until finally, he could hear the unlatching of the door. Had Pignoli actually made it? The boy could not help but tremble.

Hearing nothing further after listening for a minute or two, Hammett slowly turned the worn doorknob and pulled. He could not believe it when, indeed, he found himself standing inside of the dark *chocolaterie,* not knowing what to look for first...the mouse, the chocolate, or the lights. Suddenly, as if on cue, the *chocolaterie* lit up as Pignoli swung from the light switch, tired and sore. The little fellow had actually pulled it off.

"I *told* you to trust me," said the exhausted mouse as he let go of the switch, falling onto a stack of chocolate bars. Hammett ran to his tiny friend and gently picked him up.

"Thank you, little fellow," he whispered, stroking Pignoli's head now drenched in sweat. "Are you all right?"

"Of course," said the mouse as he climbed into Hammett's pocket, "but my work here is done. The rest is up to..." Pignoli could not finish his sentence for he had to yawn, after which he fell fast asleep once again.

"Poor little fellow," whispered the boy into his top pocket, the mouse already snoring. With his friend, once again, tucked safely away it was now time to look around...and there was plenty to see.

The *Ledoux Chocolaterie* could be considered a small shop but once inside, Hammett found himself in the midst of the most beautiful confections he had ever seen, the heavenly aroma of pure cocoa prompting him to stop and breathe in deeply, causing his mouth to water. How he wished that Trista could be there to see it all. The handmade *bonbons de chocolat* were filled with scrumptious creams, each topped with a different colored icing, while the perfectly round *mendiants* were covered with finely chopped nuts and bits of dried fruit. The fresh fragrance of citrus coming from the chocolate-dipped *orangettes* lightly wafted through the air, mixing nicely with the scent of fine caramel, so smoothly spread out and evenly cubed on a special tray. The *guimaves,* dripping with chocolate, were the largest Hammett had ever seen, but the *bouchees au chocolat* were even larger...*much* larger than Pignoli. Alongside the *pates de fruits* and the *marrons glaces* were various selections of *ganaches, pralines,* and *craquants.* Last but not least, next to the trays of pretty pink, yellow, and green *macarons,* were the *tablettes de chocolat* wrapped in flowery paper and piled high in neat stacks. Each confection was, indeed, a work of art and the boy did not know where to place his hands first.

The Ledoux Chocolaterie

Having forgotten to bring the empty flour sack that he kept in his small trunk of magic tricks for an occasion such as this, Hammett decided to stuff his pockets as best he could. But first, he would have to find the perfect treat for Pignoli. After all, the courageous mouse had not only located the *chocolaterie*, but had gotten the boy safely inside at his own peril. Perhaps a *bonbon* filled with raspberry *crème* or a chocolate drenched marshmallow would satisfy the little fellow. There was so much to choose from but, alas, the boy would not get a chance to make a choice, for a tiny pink nose came twitching out of his top pocket once again.

"I shall have a sugar-dusted fruit jelly and a candied chestnut. Oh and, of course, a chocolate covered marshmallow," the tiny mouse said before yawning. Hammett complied, stuffing the three confections into his top pocket, despite their stickiness. Pignoli made room with pleasure and wasted no time in nibbling at each one. Needless to say, it was a glorious moment.

As Pignoli contentedly bit into each of his sweet treats, every so often licking the sticky goodness from his fingers, Hammett stuffed *bonbons* into the pockets of his pants, first the lemon creams, then the raspberry, then the coconut. He stuffed as many chocolates as he could into his mouth too...so many, as a matter of fact, that his cheeks bulged as though he were a chipmunk. When he could no longer fit any more *bonbons* into either his pants or his mouth, he started grabbing as many stacks of chocolate bars as he could with both hands, forgetting that he would not only have to pick up the lantern he had placed down, but open the door to get out of the *chocolaterie*!

Satisfied with the amount of chocolate he had grabbed *and* stuffed into his mouth, Hammett figured that it was best not to be too greedy. As he slowly sauntered toward the door, swallowing the last of the delicious *bonbons*, he finally realized just how full his hands were.

"Oh my, little fellow," the boy whispered into his top pocket, "I can hardly reach for the lantern with all of these chocolate bars I am carrying." Pignoli, still licking the sugar from his fingers, was too full to poke his head out of the boy's pocket, although he would make an obvious suggestion.

"You may have to leave some of the chocolate behind," said the overstuffed mouse, burping as he rolled over in Hammett's pocket and fell, once again, into a deep slumber. The boy nodded and giggled softly to himself, for he knew that his friend was right.

"Whatever you say, little fellow," Hammett whispered. "You sleep and before you know it, we will be back at the orphanage."

But before he could put some of the chocolate bars back, Hammett heard the sound of thunderous footsteps coming down the creaky wooden stairs from the apartment above. For a split second his eyes met with those of...

"*Voleur!*" a man's voice shouted. "Thief!" Startled, the boy dropped all of the chocolate bars he had been carrying onto the floor, causing them to shatter into bits within their flowered paper wrappers...something he could do nothing about now.

With no time to lose, Hammett grabbed the lantern and threw the door open for his hands were now free, and ran down the cobblestone path, through the village square, and up the road with reckless abandon. It was not until he was dangerously out of breath that he finally stopped and collapsed off to the side of the road, coming to rest in the tall grass. Pignoli had awakened, for not only could he sense in his dreams that the boy was streaking through the night in a panic, but his tummy was upset too from all of the bouncing around...not to mention the chocolate he ate. Once again, he poked his head out of the pocket, twitching his tiny pink nose in the air.

"What happened?" asked the yawning mouse. "Why were you running so hard?"

"I...got...caught," said Hammett, breathing hard.

"Did you at least get all of the chocolate that you wanted?" Pignoli asked.

"Sort of," said the boy, still breathing hard.

"What do you mean *sort of*?" asked the confused mouse. "Either you did, or you did not."

"Well, I dropped the chocolate bars, but I still have the *bonbons*," said Hammett as he stood up and reached into his pants pockets, dredging up two sloppy fistfuls of smashed chocolates and cream. "Oh no," he lamented. "We came all this way for nothing." The boy looked as though he were about to cry.

"Nonsense!" shouted Pignoli with a finger in the air. "Trista can eat what you have there with a spoon!"

"I suppose so," the boy agreed half-heartedly. "I just wanted to give her...so much more." Unable to hide his disappointment, Hammett hung his head.

45

"So…now we have an excuse to go back!" declared the mouse. Hammett picked his head up, his eyes widening.

"Really?" he said with surprise. "You would be willing to do that after all you went through to get me into the *chocolaterie*?" Hammett could not believe his ears, having figured that their journey into the village would be a one-time adventure.

"Of course I would be willing!" declared Pignoli. "Besides, you still owe me a mouse to love…right?" The determined squeaker smiled hopefully, trusting that the boy had not forgotten.

"So I do," replied Hammett, smiling back at his tiny friend, "so I do. I must say that I *did* see several mice skittering about near the garbage cans in the back alley." Pignoli would quickly snap to attention upon hearing the boy's words. "Perhaps one of them is a *souris femelle* just waiting to meet you!"

"She would be one lucky mouse!" declared Pignoli as he licked the remaining sweetness off his fingers.

"Then it is agreed. We will return to the *chocolaterie* at a later time, but for now let us get back to Trista and the Ouble' Orphanage," Hammett said decidedly, shoving the smashed chocolates and cream back into his pockets which made him grimace. "And by the way, when we get back remind me to swipe a spoon from the kitchen."

In the meantime, back at the *chocolaterie*, Armand Ledoux was picking up the shattered chocolate bars from the shop floor. A kindly old gentleman, he and his wife Tumelo were the only chocolate makers in the village of Le Clerc, true experts who had an excellent reputation for their confections…even in Paris. Childless and getting on in years, the gentle and good couple wanted nothing more than to hand their beloved business over to someone who would love it as much as they did, someone who would carry on the tradition of the *Ledoux Chocolaterie* for years to come…and protect it from instances…such as this. But, alas, there was no one! Who would make the chocolates when they were gone? This was the question that haunted Armand and Tumelo every day, but for now all they wanted to know was…*who had broken into their chocolaterie*?

"What is it, Armand?" the sweet Tumelo asked in a tremulous voice of panic, coming down the creaky wooden stairs from the apartment above as quickly as her old legs would carry her.

"Oh, *Mon Dieu*!" cried Armand, down on his hands and knees gathering up the shattered chocolate bars. "We have had a thief,

46

my dear. Look at what he did to these chocolate bars. They are of no value now," he said sadly as Tumelo helped him to his feet. "The *bonbons* have been disturbed as well...and the chocolate covered marshmallows...and the..."

"Shhh...it is over now," Tumelo said softly, hoping to calm her husband as she took some of the shattered chocolate bars off his hands. "Did you see who it was? Did you recognize him?" she asked. Armand sat in a chair to catch his breath.

"He was a young boy, my dear Tumelo, who I have never seen before. I do not believe that he was from this village," said the kindly *chocolatier*. "Who would ever do such a thing to us?"

"No one who knows us," said Tumelo, something suddenly occurring to her. "We are not acquainted with any of the boys in the orphanage. Perhaps it was one of them." Armand became thoughtful.

"You may be right, my dear," he said. "I think I will take a ride out to the orphanage with the first morning light."

"To speak with someone in charge?" asked Tumelo.

"To catch a thief, my dear!" Armand announced with determination. "To catch a thief!"

Armand and Tumelo Ledoux

Chapter 8

The Clever Plan

Hammett returned to the Ouble' Orphanage well before the first morning light, crawling through a small window in the kitchen which he had unlocked and left slightly open. Quickly grabbing a spoon, he silently tiptoed through the corridors until he reached Trista's room, whereupon he quietly knocked on the door...once, twice, three times. Finally, after several more knocks and a number of whispered pleas, the orphan girl answered the door, rubbing her eyes.

"Hammett, is that you?" she asked.

"Trista, I have brought you something that will make you happy," said the boy, rushing into her room and closing the door, relieved to have not been caught by Signora Nonmaltobello. Putting both hands into his pockets he scooped out the shattered *bonbons*, the mixture of chocolate and cream so pleasing to the smell, but...

"Yuk! What are those ugly messes that you have taken from your pockets?" asked Trista, shuddering at the sight of the two mixed up mounds that were impossible to identify.

"It is chocolate, Trista," said Hammett. "Bonbons that got smashed up in my pockets, but I promise that they are still delicious! Take the spoon from my shirt pocket and taste," he ordered. "Go on."

Pignoli stuck his head out of the pocket and twitched his tiny pink nose high in the air for after all, he had a part in this too.

"Oh...hello," Trista said tentatively to the mouse as she removed the spoon from Hammett's shirt pocket, dipping only its tip into the crushed confections that he held in his right hand. Tasting the mixture her eyes widened with delight. Next, she took a larger spoonful and ate it...then another...then another. Finally, after so many years of sadness, the orphan girl was *smiling*.

"This is wonderful!" she declared. "Wherever did you get it?"

"At the *chocolaterie* in the village," Hammett answered, "and there is plenty more where *that* came from, only the chocolate is put together...and much prettier!" The two friends laughed.

"How did you manage to leave the orphanage without getting

caught by Signora Nonmaltobello...and how did you *ever* get into the *chocolaterie* in the middle of the night?" asked Trista. The orphan girl, who had just smiled at Hammett for the very first time after so many years of sadness, was curious and wanted to know all of the details.

"I used my wits," bragged the boy, giving himself a pat on the back. That was when Pignoli chimed in.

"Uh-hum," coughed the mouse, "remember me?"

"Oh...yes...and, of course, I could not have done it without the help of my little friend here," said Hammett, having to admit that the adventure was a *complete* success...thanks to Pignoli.

"Well, then I must thank *you*, Pignoli," said Trista, still smiling broadly as she stroked the squeaker's head with one finger.

"We will be going back to find a mouse for me to love!" he declared, proudly puffing out his tiny chest.

"A mouse for you to love?" Trista repeated with a puzzled expression, for she was unaware of the deal that Hammett had struck with Pignoli.

"I will explain the entire situation to you at breakfast tomorrow morning," the boy promised before encouraging Trista to eat the rest of the sweet chocolate and cream that he still held in the palms of his hands. She happily did so, after which time Hammett cleaned the stickiness from his fingers, glad to finally be rid of it. He felt accomplished when he finally went to bed that night, the vision of Trista's pretty smile still in his mind.

*****

Soon after sunrise just as he had planned, Armand Ledoux, the kindly *chocolatier*, left the village of Le Clerc by buggy and headed straight for the Ouble' Orphanage with the intention of catching his thief.

"Do not lose your temper, Armand," his wife Tumelo warned him, even though she had never known him to do so.

"You know I won't," he said, patting her gently on the cheek before climbing into his buggy. "Do not worry."

"I hear that the new matron can be...difficult," said Tumelo.

"How do you know that?" asked her husband as he took up the reins of his horse.

"She has been to the village to shop and, well, I have heard a few things from the villagers," confirmed the gentle old woman, embarrassed to be spreading rumors, even to her husband.

"Ahh...do not listen to gossip, my dear. I am sure that the new matron will be nice to *me*, and most cooperative as well," the kindly *chocolatier* assured his wife before nudging his horse into a steady clip-clop, clip-clop.

It was obvious that Armand Ledoux had never met Signora Nonmaltobello, for he was being far too optimistic. "I will be back by lunchtime!" he shouted over his shoulder as Tumelo waved goodbye with a white handkerchief, hoping that everything would go smoothly. But she could not help but have...a sinking feeling.

When Armand arrived at the Ouble' Orphanage, the boys and girls were gathering in the dining room for a sparse breakfast of gruel and chunks of stale bread left over from the night before. The kindly gentleman looked about the old, run-down place where little had changed since *he* was a boy, for it was there that he had lived too as an orphan...many years ago. As a matter of fact, it was there that he met an orphan girl named Tumelo, the only good thing that ever happened to him at the orphanage. Nowadays, he and his wife rarely spoke of it as so many years had passed, but it was there, indeed, that they had first met, eventually getting married when they were old enough to leave, never to look back again...until now.

"So, that is what happened, my dear Signora Nonmaltobello," said Armand, having just explained what had occurred at his *chocolaterie* the night before. "If you would be so kind as to allow me to speak with the children, I am sure that I would recognize the culprit...if he is, indeed, here." As usual, Signora Nonmaltobello, not a very nice person remember, was foul in her reply.

"You silly old man...how dare you come in here without proof? Do you actually think it is possible for any of these urchins to escape the confines of the orphanage with *me* in charge?" growled the indignant matron.

"I did not mean to imply that you have been derelict in your duties, Signora Nonmaltobello," clarified the old gentleman, "but you must admit, dear lady, that anything is possible if a person...even a child... wants it badly enough." The matron was thoughtful, but seething with anger.

"Come with me to the dining room if you must," she conceded with a nasty tone of voice, "but I defy you to find your chocolate thief there, after which I will expect a full apology."

"Agreed, dear lady, for I am a gentleman who always owns up to his mistakes," said Armand, taken aback by the matron's rudeness which he had not expected, despite Tumelo's warning.

Sticking her nose high in the air, Signora Nonmaltobello begrudgingly led the kindly *chocolatier* to the dining room where the orphans were eating their breakfast.

With Pignoli tucked safely away in his top pocket, Hammett had just sat down at a table with Trista and some of the other orphans, making the pretty blue button disappear into thin air for their entertainment. Not having seen the *chocolatier* walk in with the matron, he broke off a corner of his morsel of bread, dipped it into the bland, watery porridge, and slipped it into his pocket for the tiny mouse, now considered a hero.

It was only when Signora Nonmaltobello began to screech at the children in her usual foul manner that Hammett picked his head up, seeing her...and her familiar guest.

Without delay, he dove under the table while Pignoli remained in his pocket, calmly nibbling on his bread and porridge. Trista could not help but smile, for she found that she liked smiling again, not to mention that it was she alone who knew of Hammett's escapade the night before...she and Pignoli, that is. The scene unfolding before her was on her account and for the first time in a long time she felt...special.

"I want your attention now!" screeched Signora Nonmaltobello, clapping her hands loudly. "Stop eating and look at me!" The room fell silent. "This gentleman here owns the *chocolaterie* in the village and he *claims* that one of you may have, somehow, gained entry into his shop in the middle of the night and stolen some chocolate, leaving behind a mess of shattered chocolate bars all over the floor! Well? Will anyone own up to it?"

The orphans were dumbfounded for who could ever pull off such a stunt, especially in the middle of the night. They stood perfectly still...and silent.

As the kindly *chocolatier* scanned the room for a familiar face, Hammett remained under the table, unaware that his feet were sticking out in plain sight. Nevertheless, none of the orphans, other than Trista of course, even knew that he was under there, because all eyes were now on the gentleman standing next to the matron.

"We are in for it now," mumbled Pignoli, his mouth full of soggy bread.

"Hush! Do not speak!" Hammett ordered in a strong whisper.

Amazingly enough, however, Armand did not walk around the dining room for a closer inspection, although he *did* notice the orphan boy's feet sticking out from underneath the table. He had to think fast.

"I do apologize, dear Matron, for coming here without the necessary proof," said the kindly, old gentleman as he stared at Hammett's feet. "I must say that you have a fine group of children here at the Ouble' Orphanage."

"Yes, yes...will that be all? I no longer have the time for this nonsense!" declared Signora Nonmaltobello loudly and rudely which was just fine with Armand, for he could not wait to get out of there and away from the foul matron. But not before making a sudden and brilliant proposal.

"Yes, that will be all, my dear Signora Nonmaltobello, but I would like to say that I am so impressed with the respect shown to me by these wonderful children that I shall leave my door unlocked, day *and* night, for any orphan who would wish to pay me a visit," said the wily *chocolatier*. Upon hearing this, Hammett sprung to his knees and banged his head on the bottom of the table, causing Trista to let out a quiet giggle.

"That will not be necessary," scowled the nasty matron. "The children are not allowed to leave the premises, *and* they are *certainly* not allowed to have chocolate. It could rot their teeth and children with rotten teeth do not get adopted."

"Nevertheless, my offer still stands, dear Matron. I shall leave my door unlocked...day *and* night," Armand repeated with emphasis, loudly enough for all the orphans to hear, including Hammett. And with that, Signora Nonmaltobello had the old *chocolatier* escorted out of the Ouble' Orphanage by one of the nursemaids.

Little did she know that Armand Ledoux had just set a clever trap, for one could not always know who might be hiding...under a table.

"Did you hear that?" Hammett whispered excitedly to Pignoli. "It will be *easy* to get more chocolate, now that we know the door to the *chocolaterie* will be unlocked."

"Look out for a trick," said the smart mouse.

"Nonsense," the boy whispered into his top pocket, ignoring the warning. "There is enough oil in the lantern to go back tonight...and enough oil in the potter's shed to take us back there over and over again. As long as the *chocolatier* keeps his door unlocked, Trista will have enough chocolate to keep her happy for the rest of her life!"

Hammett was filled with joy, but Pignoli...was not so sure.

"I smell a rat," said Pignoli, "a big chocolate rat."

"Oh, do not be so doubtful," said the boy. "You should be relieved that you will no longer have to climb through the transom and make your way to the front of the shop to unlock the door for me. Besides, do you or do you not want to meet a mouse to love?"

"Well...sure I do...but," Pignoli stammered, only to be quickly interrupted.

"Then leave it all to me," said Hammett as he climbed out from underneath the table when Signora Nonmaltobello was not looking. Pignoli merely sighed, for what else could he do? The boy was stubborn and determined.

In the meantime, Armand Ledoux climbed into his buggy and headed back to the village of Le Clerc, glad to leave the orphanage behind. His smile was wide, for he knew that his plan was clever. Perhaps the culprit *was* the orphan under the table, or perhaps it was someone else, but he had the feeling that he would soon find out...maybe even tonight! He did not need Signora Nonmaltobello's help, or even her approval, for his scheme alone would be enough... to catch his thief.

Chapter 9

Allow Me This Hunch

When Armand arrived back at the *Ledoux Chocolaterie*, he found Tumelo anxiously awaiting his return. He told her all about his woeful visit to the Ouble' Orphanage.

"Not much has changed for the poor children who live there, my dear," he said with sadness.

"Do not speak of it," his wife answered somberly, "for it brings back such unpleasant memories. If only we could help...even one of them."

"First things first, my dear," answered Armand. "Remember that I have a chocolate thief to catch, and I am all but certain that he lives at the orphanage."

"Really?" Tumelo gasped, her eyes now wide with curiosity.

"Let me explain everything from the beginning," said Armand as he went on to tell his wife all about the feet he saw sticking out from underneath the table when he walked into the dining room, this causing her to chuckle.

"Why did you not take hold of the two feet and drag the child out from his hiding place?" asked Tumelo with a smile. "If you are so determined to catch this thief, then I do not understand why..."

"The reason is simple, my dear Tumelo," Armand interrupted. "You were right about the matron, for she is quite difficult...to say the least." Armand rolled his eyes and made an unpleasant face. "If I were to drag that child out from underneath the table and he turned out to be innocent...just a scamp playing hide and seek...Signora Nonmaltobello would have humiliated me in front of the rest of the children, not to mention how horrible I would have felt for the innocent orphan under the table!" Armand was thoughtful before taking his wife's hand. "When we left the orphanage all those years ago, my dear," he began softly, "I vowed that I would never again allow a matron to humiliate me."

"I remember, Armand," said the kindly old Tumelo as she gently patted her husband's hand, "but what will you do now? How can you be certain that your chocolate thief lives at the orphanage, and if you *become* certain, how will you catch him?"

"By being clever, dear wife. I have a plan!" the proud *chocolatier* announced before quickly walking up to their apartment above the shop. Tumelo called after him, wondering what in the world he was up to, but before long her husband had appeared once again...with a cot.

"What are you doing with that silly old bed?" asked Tumelo.

"I shall sleep right here in the shop until the chocolate thief returns!" Armand revealed.

"What makes you think that he will return?" Tumelo asked, afraid that her husband had lost his mind. Armand smiled broadly as he explained the plan to his wife, for he thought it to be quite clever and was certain that it would work. Tumelo listened carefully...and thoughtfully.

"Do you think it is wise, dear husband, to leave the door to the chocolaterie unlocked, day and night?" she asked.

"It is most certainly wise, my dear, for it guarantees the return of our chocolate thief," Armand assured his wife, "as long as he, indeed, lives at the Ouble' Orphanage...which I believe he does."

"And what if he does not?" asked Tumelo with her hands on her hips.

"Then I shall drift off to sleep every night with the heavenly aroma of chocolate confections swirling around inside of my head!" laughed the amused chocolatier who clearly aimed to carry out his plan...no matter what his dear wife said. But it did not take him long to get serious again. "Allow me this hunch, Tumelo," he said earnestly, "for I have a feeling that those feet sticking out from underneath the table this morning were the same feet that ran out of here last night." Tumelo smiled and turned to walk up the stairs to their apartment. "Where are you going, my dear?" asked the chocolatier.

"To get blankets and a pillow for the cot," she answered. And with that Armand smiled, for he knew that Tumelo had allowed him...his hunch.

*****

In the meantime, Hammett devised a plan to return to the chocolaterie that evening, despite Pignoli's objections.

"The chocolatier is a sly old fox," said the smug mouse as he nibbled on a dried-up pea that Hammett had found on the floor... underneath the table.

"Why do you say that?" asked the boy.

"I say it because his plan to leave the door to the *chocolaterie* unlocked day *and* night is quite shrewd," said Pignoli, smacking his lips, "and you fell for it."

"What do you mean by that?" Hammett asked.

"Oh, come now," said the tiny squeaker, wise beyond his years. "Do you not see it for what it is...a mere ploy to get you back into his shop?"

"Nonsense," Hammett repeated, once again ignoring his friend's warning. "He is just an old man being nice. Besides, he does not know me...he barely saw me."

"But he has, somehow, figured out that the culprit lives *here*," said Pignoli.

"For a mouse, you are quite the scaredy cat," said the smiling boy. "Oh well...come with me or stay behind...it no longer matters, for I now know how to get there *and* how to get in, no help required. Then again, there is the matter of those little white mice in the back alley," he said artfully. Hammett knew that he could wear Pignoli down simply by mentioning the one thing that the tiny white squeaker so desperately longed for...a mouse to love.

"All right, all right," said the little fellow, throwing his tiny hands up in the air. "You have talked me into going, but if you get caught..."

"Then I shall personally see to it that you are given a home in the back alley," interrupted the boy, waving his hand. "Just trust me."

Pignoli was not as confident as Hammett was, for he was certain that the *chocolatier* would be waiting for them. But...he had to take the chance. After all, a good adventure was worth the risk, especially if it could lead to his heart's desire.

That afternoon, the orphans were told that out of the goodness of his heart, and a touch of pity, the local abbe' would be providing them with dinner that evening...ham, *potatoes au gratin*, and a dessert that Hammett had never had before—ice cream. The boy knew that he could not pass up such a feast, for that kind of a meal was unheard of at the Ouble' Orphanage. The *chocolaterie* would have to wait. Besides, perhaps it was wise to avoid tempting the fates again so soon. After all, he had just sneaked past the sleeping nursemaid only the night before. It would not hurt to wait one more day, and his stomach would thank him for it. So would Pignoli.

That evening the orphans made merry, for the food was good and plentiful. Gobbling it up as though it would disappear, they ate and ate until they could no longer do so, their bellies quite full for the first time... ever. After devouring the main meal, leaving only a hambone, they indulged in the sweet ice cream that had been hand-churned at the convent creamery by the nuns of St. Claire. Hammett felt as though he were in heaven, and Pignoli had not done so bad either, having had a bit of ham fat and a lick of ice cream off of the boy's finger.

"I am *so* full," said Hammett, rubbing his belly.

"Me too," said the mouse from the boy's pocket, likewise rubbing his own belly as the fun continued.

After waiting for a few minutes to digest his food, Hammett walked over to the table where the abbe' was sitting with Signora Nonmaltobello to thank him for the wonderful meal. The old priest was appreciative of the boy's politeness...and his talent. Hammett did magic tricks for him, making his fork disappear, pulling a franc from behind his ear, and pulling a bouquet of flowers from the sleeve of his long, black jacket. The abbe' laughed and clapped, delighted by what the orphan boy could do, but Signora Nonmaltobello was decidedly unimpressed, or at least she appeared to be, for she refused to give the boy even a slight hint of approval.

The next evening, Hammett and Pignoli departed for the village once again, having already left the same window in the kitchen partially open and gone past the sleeping nursemaid who was snoring rather loudly...as usual. The daring orphan boy and his mouse, each determined to get what he wanted, used the lantern sparingly this time, for they now knew their way into the village square and from there...to the *chocolaterie*. The moon was full and bright, guiding them for much of the way. The two friends were in the village before they knew it.

"Someday, I will walk the streets of this village in broad daylight," declared Hammett, "and Trista will be right by my side."

"And I shall be in your pocket," Pignoli said, "with...with...with someone by *my* side too...will I not?" asked the mouse, stammering his words.

"Of course you will," confirmed the boy. "You need not worry about that."

In the meantime, Armand lay comfortably on his cot, which he had placed behind a partition in a dark corner of the *chocolaterie*. Tumelo had made it comfortable for him with a soft blanket and their best feather pillow. The kindly old man read a book by candlelight as he quietly lay there, but he was getting sleepy as the hour was late, causing him to think that the chocolate thief would, once again, fail to come. He closed his book and blew out the candle, still able to see a soft glow of light coming from the rest of the shop. Contented and warm on the cot, he breathed in the fragrance of freshly made chocolate confections, so soothing to the smell, before passing into a pleasant sleep.

On this second night of his sleeping in the shop, Armand was in a comfortable slumber, but before his dreams could even begin, he awoke to the sound of someone walking through the unlocked door of the *chocolaterie* and switching on the light. He quietly got up from his cot and peered out from behind the partition at the young stranger, relieved that his clever plan had indeed worked, for the intruder's shoes...he easily recognized. The old man chose to simply *watch* the orphan boy for now as he looked around the *chocolaterie*, studying the designs of the beautiful confections. He walked from glass case to glass case, slowly and deliberately this time rather than quickly and haphazardly like the last time. There was no grabbing or seizing or clutching...no clasping or grasping... and no frenzied stuffing of chocolates into his mouth. The boy seemed to appreciate the beauty of each and every chocolate, and Armand proudly enjoyed watching him.

"Look at how pretty these chocolates are, Pignoli," Hammett said with wonder as he studied each one. "What a talented man the *chocolatier* is...and how artistic!" The tiny mouse poked his head out from the boy's top pocket, reluctant at having to take a tour of the shop.

"Just grab your chocolate and let us get out of here," he directed in a scared voice. "I have a funny feeling we are being watched."

"Nonsense," said Hammett, his usual way of answering the mouse lately. "There is so much to look at...so much to explore. I cannot believe that I neglected to notice the beauty of the *chocolatier's* work the first time we were here!"

"You said that we would go to the back alley and look for..." Pignoli began.

"Yes, yes," Hammett interrupted with the usual wave of his hand. "There is plenty of time for that." Absolutely charmed by what he saw, he made a wistful comment. "Oh, what I would not give to spend my days...in a place like this."

The wide-eyed boy looked around a little more before picking up a rag. Carefully and gently he cleaned the top of every glass case in the shop while Armand watched his young chocolate thief from behind the partition with inexplicable delight...rather than anger. The boy rubbed out every smudge and fingerprint better than Tumelo ever could, and he dusted the tables and shelves too, moving the chocolate around most carefully and with a new found respect. Once everything glistened, making the beautiful chocolate confections themselves sparkle like jewels, he took hold of a broom that stood in the corner. He swept the floor, picking up the little bit of dust that he had gathered with his two hands, and tossed it out the front door of the shop.

"What do you think you are doing?" asked Pignoli.

"Just cleaning up a bit," said Hammett, "as payment for the last time we were here. And when we come back..."

"Come back!" the mouse blurted out.

"Yes, come back...I shall clean the windows inside and out," he said.

"Whatever for?" the annoyed squeaker asked.

"To pretend I suppose...and wish...that a place such as this could be mine one day. It would make Trista happy for the rest of her life." Hammett had a far-away look in his eye.

"But it is not yours *now*," stressed Pignoli, "so let us get out of here before we get caught!"

"All right, all right," Hammett agreed, putting only one bonbon in his mouth while taking three chocolate bars. "I have all that I want for now."

"Are you kidding me?" asked the mouse. "After the work you did, that is all you are taking?"

"For now," repeated the boy. "We will come back soon." He looked around the shop with great admiration, proud of the work he had done. "It is time to go to the back alley, my friend."

"Finally," Pignoli mumbled anxiously. "Now you are talking."

Hammett walked to the front door of the *chocolaterie* and stopped, turning around for one last look. "Yes, I really do like this place," he whispered before walking out, quietly closing the door behind him. Armand appeared from behind the partition, unsure of what he had just seen while at the same time, Tumelo came down the old, wooden stairs from the apartment above.

"Armand, I heard a voice," she yawned sleepily. "Did you catch our chocolate thief?"

"No, my dear," Armand answered with a shake of his head, unable to explain to his wife what had just happened. He simply had no words.

"Then what was that voice I heard?" Tumelo asked.

"I must have been talking in my sleep," he said, looking around at his splendidly clean shop. "Go back to bed, dear Tumelo, for morning will be here soon enough." The kindly old woman nodded in agreement, kissing her husband on the forehead before heading back up the stairs.

Once he was alone again, Armand paced the floor. He knew that this was no ordinary chocolate thief, for he seemed to *belong* in the shop...*and* care about it. The puzzled *chocolatier* scratched his head. *Juste Ciel*! Could it be that one day this boy might actually help him, perhaps even take over the shop?

It was late and Armand began to think that his thoughts were crazy, probably brought on by sleepiness. After all, the boy *was* a thief...with familiar shoes! He walked back to his cot behind the partition to lie down, certain that if the boy *were* to ever work for him, he would demand to know why he talked so much...into his top pocket. And with that, Armand let out a soft chuckle and blocked out any further thoughts. He drifted off into a deep and sound sleep, anticipating the next time he would see...his chocolate thief.

Chapter 10

The Back Alley

Thoroughly satisfied with his visit to the *chocolaterie*, Hammett strolled around the corner to the back alley, looking to find a mouse for Pignoli to love. There he saw the usual garbage and empty crates, a genuine paradise for rodents...a dream come true for his tiny friend.

"You may see a rat or two," Hammett warned as Pignoli calmly washed his face with both hands.

"I pay them no mind," said the mouse nonchalantly. "Such bossy creatures the way they push themselves into places they do not belong. They always insist upon being the first ones to belly up to the garbage cans too, simply because they are a little larger and their tails a little longer." Hammett could not help but smile. "So rude," Pignoli continued, shaking his head, "*and* silly. You will *never* find me giving a rat the time of day." He continued to groom himself, buffing his two front teeth on the cloth of Hammett's shirt pocket, and carefully smoothing back the fur on his head. "I am ready now," he said with an official tone of voice, the look on his face quite solemn.

"You seem a bit nervous," said Hammett.

"Not at all...just...*prepared*," said the mouse.

"All right, my friend," giggled the boy. "Let us find you a mouse..."

"To love!" Pignoli chimed in, poking his head out of Hammett's top pocket as the two walked at their leisure through the feast of food scraps and other discarded things. But something caused the mouse to jump with fright. "Is that a person?" he asked, visibly trembling.

"That is merely a broken mannequin," Hammett calmly assured his friend, the dim light of the lantern throwing off nighttime shadows that danced and played tricks on Pignoli. Reaching into his top pocket, he gently stroked the head of the tiny mouse to calm him. "Do not worry, little fellow," the boy whispered. "As long as you are with me, you are safe. Now let me see," he quietly uttered to himself, trying to determine exactly *where* he had seen the mice on their first venture into the back alley. "Ah yes...I believe I was standing over there...near the garbage cans...beside the crates...close to the rotten lettuce and tomatoes."

Hammett silently tiptoed over to the exact spot he had just pinpointed and stood there.

"Now what?" Pignoli asked.

"Now this!" declared the boy as he quickly picked up one of the crates while lifting a loosely placed lid off of the nearest garbage can at the same time. Two plump, brown rats hastily scurried out of the can while a group of three white mice, all of them baring a striking resemblance to Pignoli, remained where the crate had been, nibbling on spoiled strawberries and pears. "Voila!" Hammett announced triumphantly.

Unafraid and quite hungry, the three white mice stayed perfectly in place as they ate their fruit, while Pignoli watched from the boy's top pocket...a safe distance away. He looked at Hammett and smiled anxiously.

"Let me down slowly," whispered the mouse, licking his lips and twitching his tiny pink nose.

"Are you sure?" Hammett asked.

"Quite sure," Pignoli said confidently. "Besides, I am starving and that fruit looks pretty good."

"All right, my friend," said the boy who was now more nervous than the mouse. "If you are quite sure, then down you shall go."

Gently lifting Pignoli, who now looked quite dapper after having groomed himself, out of his top pocket, Hammett carefully placed him on the ground at his feet. Throwing caution to the wind, the tiny squeaker skittled over to the three mice that were still eating their strawberries and pears. They instantly stopped and demanded an explanation from this unfamiliar intruder, this stranger to the back alley.

"Who are you?" asked the largest mouse, disgruntled by the interruption of his meal.

"I am Pignoli from the village of Arancia, now in residence at the Ouble' Orphanage," said the squeaker, his eyes fixed on the pretty little mouse to his left.

"Aren't *you* the proper fellow," he sneered. "Well, go away Pignoli from the village of Arancia. There is no place for you here. Arancian mice are...pushy." But Pignoli ignored his insult.

"I was hoping to share your meal and, perhaps...make a new friend," he said, still staring at the pretty little mouse to his left.

She looked back at him and smiled sweetly, causing his heart to suddenly go aflutter.

"Find your *own* meal," said the large, rude mouse. "There is only enough fruit for *us*. Besides, my sister, brother, and I were here first."

"That is correct," agreed the younger of the two brothers. "We cannot spare a single bite, especially for a mouse from...Arancia."

"Hey, what do the two of you have against Arancia?" Pignoli asked, now annoyed as he raised his two tiny fists.

"Oh...a fighter, are you?" commented the larger mouse. "I knew you would be *pushy*."

"A real troublemaker," said his younger brother, leering at Pignoli.

"Enough!" the pretty little mouse ordered her two siblings. "I have told you both time and again...if you can say nothing nice, then remain silent!" The two brothers scowled at their sister at first but eventually took her scolding to heart, backing away from Pignoli and scattering into the shadows.

Just like that, quicker than the snap of two fingers, Pignoli and the pretty little mouse that stood to his left were suddenly alone.

"I must apologize for my brothers," she said shyly. "They can sometimes be...unkind."

"Oh, that is all right," answered Pignoli who blushed a bright red, the sweet exchange tickling Hammett who was watching from a nearby doorway, thankful for the success of their adventure so far!

"Please join me for strawberries and pears," said the pretty little mouse, her invitation most welcomed by Pignoli.

"Do not mind if I do," he said, scurrying over to the spoiled fruit before she could change her mind. "How kind of you to invite me."

"Oh, my pleasure...Pignoli is it?" she said politely, continuing to nibble her fruit.

"From Arancia," he repeated.

"Yes, I heard," she answered shyly before letting out a sweet giggle. Pignoli was smitten.

"And what is your name?" he asked.

"I am Fleur, originally from Paris," said the gentle mouse before properly wiping her little mouth with a scrap of clean napkin. "How did you get to Le Clerc all the way from Arancia?"

"I came by train," said Pignoli, sticking out his chest. "It is the only way for an intelligent mouse such as myself to travel."

"My brothers and I stowed away in the buggy wheel of a rich businessman who happened to be traveling from Paris to Le Clerc, and this back alley has been our home ever since," said Fleur. "The food is plentiful, but it sometimes gets lonely here."

"I live at the Ouble' Orphanage where the food is sparse, but it *never* gets lonely," commented Pignoli.

"Do you mean to tell me that you are around people all day long?" the impressed mouse asked. "You are lucky! Other than the men who occasionally pick up the garbage, no one ever comes back *here*...until now, that is," she said in her shy little voice, curiously looking over at Hammett.

"Oh...please allow me to introduce you to my good friend," said Pignoli, noticing Fleur's interest in the boy who eagerly stepped forward.

"Hello, dear lady," he said immediately, bowing like a true gentleman. "I am Hammett of the Ouble' Orphanage."

"Hello to *you*, sir," said Fleur, curtsying as beautifully as any little mouse ever could. The boy bent down and picked up the two newly acquainted squeakers.

"It is a pleasure to meet you," he said. "I heard you say that it sometimes gets lonely back here."

"Other than my brothers, kind sir, I have no one else to speak to," said Fleur.

"Do you not have a single friend to call your own?" Hammett asked. The boy felt genuinely sorry for the pretty little mouse for she was such an amicable creature...unlike her two boorish brothers.

"The chance to make a friend has never presented itself until now," she said, smiling demurely at Pignoli.

"Well, now you have *two* friends, dear mouse, and if on this night you choose to come with us, I promise that you will never be lonely again," proposed Hammett.

"I could *not* leave my brothers, kind sir," said the flustered little mouse, dismissing the idea with a wave of her hand until...

"Oh, but you *can*," said Fleur's large, rude brother as he skittled out of the shadows, the younger brother dutifully following. "We overheard your conversation and have decided that it would be best for *us*," he said, pointing to himself and his brother, "to leave the back alley on the next fruit and vegetable wagon, freeing you to do as you please." The two brothers had inexplicably exchanged their rudeness for kindness and wanted to speak with their sister. Hammett gently lowered Fleur back to the ground.

"Of course, we shall miss you," said the younger brother, "but a fruit and vegetable truck is no place for a little lady such as yourself... it would be far too dangerous."

"As much as we hate to admit it," said the older brother, squinting his eyes at Pignoli who promptly squinted back, "you would be much better off with Hammett of the Ouble' Orphanage and his little pet here...Pignoli of Arancia." This comment caused Pignoli to put up his two tiny fists once again, ready to defend his honor.

"Now, now," Hammett whispered, gently calming his friend. "That will not be necessary." The boy could easily see that things were going their way.

"Are you sure?" asked Fleur, who could not help but smile.

"Quite sure," said the older brother. "You must *never* turn down the friendship of a human...*ever*," he advised his sister before backing away. "Goodbye, dear Fleur, and good luck!" he shouted as the two brothers skittled into the shadows once again. Fleur gratefully waved goodbye, now free to start a new life.

"Hey, I am not a pet!" Pignoli shouted after them, even though they were already...long gone.

"Put your twitchy pink nose back in joint, little fellow," the boy laughed, gently petting his insulted friend before picking Fleur up off the ground once again. "It is time to go home." Pignoli cooled down quickly and let out his mousiest giggle, for he knew it would be silly to remain offended during this...the happiest time of his entire skittle-skattle life.

Hammett smiled broadly, dropping *two* joyous mice into his top pocket, for the adventure into the back alley had been a great success! Taking up his lantern, he began the long walk back to the Ouble' Orphanage as Pignoli and Fleur talked and laughed, enjoying each other's company while getting to know each other. Yes, they were happy mice indeed, for the pretty little Fleur would never be lonely again. And Pignoli had finally found...a mouse to love!

Pignoli and Fleur

Chapter 11

The Same Feet, the Same Shoes...the Same Boy

After a sound sleep, Armand awoke refreshed and thoughtful. He would have to tell Tumelo all that had happened the night before...how the boy who talked into his top pocket came into the *chocolaterie* and closely studied the designs of their beautiful confections; how he picked up a rag and cleaned the top of every glass case better than she ever could; how he dusted the tables and shelves ever so carefully so as not to damage the delicate chocolates that so daintily sat upon them; and how he took hold of the broom that stood in the corner and swept the floor, picking up the dust that he had gathered with his two bare hands. Yes...he took a *bonbon* and three chocolate bars, not to mention what he had stolen on his previous visit, but the *chocolatier* could not forget the boy's words: *Oh, what I would not give to spend my days in a place like this.*

Such a statement touched Armand for he was keenly aware that without a son or daughter he would need a successor, someone willing to someday take over the *Ledoux Chocolaterie*. Not just anyone, mind you, but someone who would be forever devoted to a lifetime of chocolate making, who would carry on the *Ledoux* tradition. Armand had an idea...but would Tumelo like it?

"Tumelo, my dear," he began delicately, "we have had a wonderful life together, have we not?"

"Oh, yes, dear Armand, we certainly *have* had a wonderful life together," agreed Tumelo.

"We have always been quite fortunate, have we not?" asked the *chocolatier*.

"Yes, quite fortunate," answered his dear wife, nodding her head.

"Then perhaps it is time to share that good fortune with someone else," Armand said gently.

"What is this all about?" Tumelo asked, wondering for a moment why Armand was asking questions...until it dawned on her. "Does this have something to do with our chocolate thief?"

Armand became animated and told Tumelo everything that had

happened the night before...how the boy who talked into his top pocket came into the *chocolaterie* and closely studied the designs of their beautiful confections; how he picked up a rag and cleaned the top of every glass case better than she ever could; how he dusted the tables and shelves ever so carefully so as not to damage the delicate chocolates that so daintily sat upon them; and how he took hold of the broom that stood in the corner and swept the floor, picking up the dust that he had gathered with his two bare hands. Last, but certainly not least, Armand repeated to Tumelo, with tears in his eyes, what the boy had said: *Oh, what I would not give to spend my days in a place like this.*

"So you see, my dear Tumelo, why I would want to share our good fortune with this boy. He can start here as an apprentice and then eventually...become our successor," said the *chocolatier*, who took in a deep breath and held it.

"But he is a thief, Armand!" Tumelo reminded him. "You want to feed and clothe a boy who has stolen from us, not just once but twice, and then leave our beloved *chocolaterie* to him when we are gone? Where is your outrage, dear husband?"

"My dear, you did not see what I saw, or hear what I heard. Besides, who are we to turn away the help of...a fellow orphan?" asked Armand, his tone suddenly softening. "I am sure you remember how lonely it was there, how..."

"Yes, yes," said Tumelo, not really wanting to recall her childhood, "I remember, but how can you be sure that he is actually from the Ouble' Orphanage?"

"Let us just say that I got a glimpse of his feet *and* the shoes he was wearing," said Armand.

"Were they the same feet you saw sticking out from underneath the table at the orphanage?" Tumelo asked, her eyes now widening with curiosity.

"The same feet, the same shoes...the same boy," he confirmed.

"I do not know if what you suggest is fitting, dear husband," Tumelo lamented, shaking her head in doubt.

"I will make a deal with you," Armand said to his skeptical wife. "You await his return along *with* me and observe him for yourself. If you do not like what you see or hear, then I will forget about my idea entirely. However, if you are as touched by this boy as I am, then..."

"Then we shall discuss it further," Tumelo said to her husband, placing a gentle hand on his. The *chocolatier* would have to be satisfied with his dear wife's response...for now.

*****

In the meantime, Hammett made Fleur comfortable in her new home, fixing up a special place inside his small trunk of magic tricks. Pignoli was much more contented to stay underneath the boy's pillow or inside his pocket. He would never *dream* of living in the small trunk, but Fleur was thoroughly delighted.

"Thank you, kind sir," said the pretty little mouse. "This is the most agreeable home I have ever had."

"You are most welcome, dear Fleur," said the boy politely with a bow. "I am here to serve you." Suddenly, Pignoli climbed up Hammett's arm and onto his shoulder. Without hesitation, the tiny mouse stood straight up and bit the boy's ear. "Ouch!" cried Hammett. "Why did you do that?"

"No need to be so...courteous," said the jealous mouse.

"Nonsense," said the boy. "There are more important things to worry about."

"Such as?" asked the annoyed mouse.

"Such as our next trip to the *chocolaterie*," Hammett reminded him.

Pignoli stuck his tongue out at the boy before washing his face with both hands. He then skittled over to the small trunk of magic tricks to keep company with Fleur, not wanting to even *think* about another nighttime trip into the village. But, Hammett...had started making his plans.

Pacing the floor of his tiny room a number of times...back and forth, back and forth...Hammett plotted his next visit to the *Ledoux Chocolaterie*, which he anticipated would be the best visit of all. The only problem was that whenever he paced, he could never keep his thoughts to himself, jabbering on and on rather loudly... enough to be overheard by Signora Nonmaltobello, who had just so happened to be sneakily passing by, listening for a reason to stop and eavesdrop at the closed door.

"We shall leave tomorrow night after darkness falls," said Hammett, rubbing his two hands together. "I will sneak out to the potter's shed tomorrow morning to get more oil for the lantern or,

70

perhaps, get another lantern all together! Yes...that would be best... another lantern...already *filled* with oil. Oh, and the window in the kitchen must be left unlocked before we leave so that we can get back in...or should I leave it open?"

The boy's thoughts came tumbling out of his mouth as soon as they entered his brain. Pignoli and Fleur watched him pace...back and forth, back and forth...their little heads turning left then right as they followed his steps.

"I feel like I am watching a ping pong match," Pignoli commented. Fleur placed a hand over her mouth and stifled a giggle.

"I think it is rather funny," she said. Pignoli rolled his eyes.

"What would my role be this time?" Pignoli asked, interrupting the boy's train of thought. "You already know how to get to the *chocolaterie*, and its front door will surely be unlocked again. What is left for me to do?"

"You will be my lookout little fellow, my assistant. You too, Fleur," Hammett said quickly before going back to his planning, once again saying out loud what he was thinking. "We will sneak out the front door of the orphanage just like before, right under the nose of that foolish sleeping nursemaid. Oh yes...it is all coming together now."

The boy smiled, feeling confident in his plan until he heard a noise outside of his bedroom door. His head snapped around, and he carefully trained his eyes on the doorknob. "Pignoli!" he called out in a throaty whisper.

"Say no more," the mouse said calmly, raising a tiny hand.

Pignoli jumped out of the small trunk of magic tricks and scurried over to the door, sticking his small head underneath. With only his twitchy pink nose and beady little eyes showing, he found himself looking up at Signora Nonmaltobello, her brow furrowed and her ear pressed tightly to the door.

The squeaker quickly backed up and skittled over to Hammett. He stood on his two hind legs and held his belly while giggling a tiny mouse giggle. "It is you know who...standing you know where... listening to you know what," said the mouse with a silly laugh, barely able to get his words out.

"Oh, is that so," Hammett whispered, knowing now that he would have to change his plan. For good measure he knocked loudly on the door, sending the snooping matron backwards, landing her right on her rump with a great big thud. He stifled a laugh, and then quickly opened the door.

"Dear lady!" the boy shouted, rushing over to help her off the floor. "Are you all right? I heard a loud noise and here you are...on the floor! How awful for you!"

Mindful of the fact that she could never admit to having her ear to the door, although the boy's impertinent knock had indicated to her that he already knew, the matron concocted a quick excuse in an attempt to appear the innocent victim of an accidental fall.

"I tripped," she said curtly, knowing that the boy's words were only a false show of concern...a mockery...for she had obviously been caught. "It is none of your business anyway!"

The embarrassed matron dusted herself off before speaking again. "Go back to whatever it is you were doing! You have taken up enough of my time!"

Of course, she would never admit to him that she had overheard everything, but it was all safely tucked away in her head...*tomorrow night when darkness falls...the potter's shed tomorrow morning... open window in the kitchen...sneak out the front door under the nose of the sleeping nursemaid.*

Signora Nonmaltobello quickly stalked down the hallway as she talked to herself, her heavy footsteps storming an angry path. "So he thinks he is going to the *chocolaterie* in the village," she mumbled and grumbled. "I will catch him in the act before he even has the chance to leave the Ouble' Orphanage!"

And with that, the foul matron disappeared from sight. Hammett smiled and went back into his bedroom, quickly slamming the door.

"There has been a change of plans!" the boy announced. "I am sure that she knows everything. We must find another time and another way to leave the orphanage...to avoid getting caught."

"This will take some thought," commented Pignoli, "and I cannot think on an empty stomach."

"All right, all right. Give me a little time and I will find you something to eat," said Hammett. "Perhaps there is a crumb or two on the dining room floor."

But before the boy could leave his room to head down to the dining room, he was stopped by a sudden knock on the door. Thinking that it must be Signora Nonmaltobello again, he opened the door apprehensively, only to find Trista standing there. It suddenly occurred to him that she was the only orphan who had a bedroom window that faced the road…leading to the village! The key to his plan stood right in front of him!

Wondering why he had not thought of it before, he pulled her into his room and quickly closed the door. "Trista, I need your help," the boy said desperately. "We need to make a plan."

Pignoli skittled back to the small trunk of magic tricks and sat beside Fleur. The two mice watched and listened carefully as Hammett and Trista made their plans.

"Interesting," Fleur commented.

"Do you really think so?" Pignoli asked. "Frankly, I am too hungry to concentrate on it any further." The tiny white mouse proceeded to wash his face before settling down for a nap, knowing that his snack would now be a long…way…off.

Hammett and Trista

Chapter 12

Moonlight and Star Shine

Trista was more than happy to grant Hammett access to her bedroom window that faced the road leading to the village, especially if it meant that he would be returning with more chocolate. As a matter of fact, as the two friends planned Hammett's next trip, the orphan girl was still eating the chocolate bar he had slipped into her hands under the breakfast table that morning.

Careful not to let anyone see what he had given her, *especially* Signora Nonmaltobello, she had quickly dropped the precious gift into the large pocket of her worn out dress, nibbling on it every so often...when no one was looking, of course. Now, she had just about finished with it, even the last bits of chocolate lighting up her face with a smile that would stay for a long time.

As they talked, Hammett merrily juggled, stood on his head, and did card tricks, for he had not only made his Trista happy, but he would be returning to the *Ledoux Chocolaterie*. He excitedly told her again about this wonderful place, describing in detail the artistic confections and how he had cleaned and swept up the shop, secretly wishing that it would one day be his. Could such a dream... possibly come true? The orphan girl listened with a happy heart, but then suddenly became thoughtful.

"Are you lonely when you walk into the village by yourself at night?" she asked.

"I was at first," said Hammett, "but not anymore."

"The next time you go, may I come with you?" Trista asked, still smiling. "I would very much like to see this *chocolaterie* of yours." Hammett's heart skipped a beat.

"Of course you may go with me!" he exclaimed. "I would love for you to see it!" The boy could not have asked for a nicer surprise and no one, not even the foul matron, could spoil it for him.

In the meantime, if Signora Nonmaltobello thought that she could catch the chocolate thief before he left the orphanage based on the information she had overheard...she was wrong.

Hammett and Trista devised a plan that would completely throw her off the track. No matter how carefully she watched...or looked...or listened, the foul matron could find no hint of what she had secretly learned. As a matter of fact, she did not detect *any* sneaking around at all...to the potter's shed for lantern oil, past the sleeping matron to get out, or through an unlocked kitchen window to get back in.

Three days and nights would pass, making it appear to her that the orphan boy's talk of a nighttime trip into the village was merely gibberish, until on the fourth night...a full moon appeared.

"See, I told you," said Trista, looking out from her bedroom window. "When the moon is your guide, then there is no need for a lantern." The orphan girl could not have been more correct, for beams of moonlight and star shine gloriously illuminated the road and its surrounding countryside. It was a perfect night...for chocolate.

Hammett was enchanted by Trista's knowledge and embarrassed that he himself had not thought of traveling by moonlight. With Pignoli and Fleur tucked safely into his top pocket, he climbed out easily from the first-floor bedroom window, followed closely by Trista who was looking forward to her first trip *ever* into the village of Le Clerc.

"Do you mean to tell me that you have *never* been to the village, even as a small child?" Hammett asked after regaining his footing under the large window.

"Both my parents died when I was three," said Trista, having landed just fine on both feet. "I have no memory of them *or* the village." The two friends began their journey, the orphan girl walking with a skip in her step as she spoke, for the freedom of the open air suited her. "Had *you* ever been to the village before coming to the Ouble' Orphanage?" she asked.

"I *think* so," said Hammett, wrinkling his nose, "but my memory is hazy. It is Pignoli here who gets all of the credit for taking me on my first *real* adventure into the village. I would have never even *found* the *chocolaterie* if it had not been for him." The tiny white mouse poked his head out of the boy's top pocket and smiled. Hammett gently stroked the smooth white fur on the top of his head, for he appreciated all that his little friend had done for him. And now that Pignoli had a mouse to love, the feeling was...quite mutual.

Although their conversation was relaxed, trouble was brewing that would cloud the moonlight and star shine, for without their knowledge, the two orphan friends were being watched as they embarked upon the winding road that would eventually lead them into the village of Le Clerc. The shadowy figure of Signora Nonmaltobello stood in the attic window of the orphanage, looking down upon them and seething with anger, for she had been tricked. Taking in a deep breath she blew hard on her whistle, summoning a large brigade of nursemaids and groundskeepers.

"Go after them," she hissed in her most foul manner, "and bring them back to me." Her mood was dark and she planned a swift and heavy-handed punishment for the escaped orphans once they were returned to her clutches. But for now, all she could do...was wait.

In the meantime, Tumelo was trying to talk Armand into coming back upstairs to sleep. "Three nights have passed, dear husband, and the boy has still not returned. Why not forget about this chocolate thief for now and come back upstairs where you will be much more comfortable."

"I cannot forget about him," said Armand. "Besides, I have a funny feeling that he will show up here tonight."

"How can you be certain of that?" Tumelo asked him.

"Tonight is the full moon, my dear wife, and magical things happen during the full moon," the *chocolatier* said with confidence. "You will see...I promise." The kindly old woman remained with her husband in the darkness of the shop, awaiting magical things, awaiting...their chocolate thief.

Hammett and Trista were not long on their journey to the village before they realized that they were being followed.

"You must go back to the orphanage before they catch up to us," Hammett warned before he and Trista ducked behind a thick wall of leafy bushes. The orphan girl was hesitant.

"I will not go back without you," she answered, her voice filled with alarm.

"You must," the boy insisted. "I do not want you to get caught. Just cut through those trees and you will be back at the orphanage before you know it."

"I do not want *you* to get caught either," Trista whispered. "How will you avoid it?"

"I will run all the way to the village, through the village square, down the alleyway, and then straight to the *chocolaterie*. Signora Nonmaltobello's thugs will never catch up to me," Hammett said confidently. "Go now and do not worry, for I will not only avoid getting caught, but I will most certainly return with more chocolate...

to make you happy." Trista was not so sure this time.

"Perhaps you *should* go back," Pignoli said to Hammett as he suddenly poked his head out of the boy's top pocket. The mouse stretched and yawned before looking around, his tiny pink nose twitching high in the air. "I smell trouble," he said cautiously.

"Nonsense," Hammett said with a smirk. "I am going forward and it is Trista who is going back to the orphanage...without me," he said, gesturing to the orphan girl. "And *you* are going back to sleep," he ordered Pignoli, gently pushing him back into his top pocket.

"We must move...now!" said Hammett. Trista finally agreed.

As she cut through the trees and headed back toward the Ouble' Orphanage, Hammett ran at full speed to the village. Through the village square he darted and swerved, avoiding the fruit and vegetable carts that were cloaked in darkness, for he knew now where they stood. As he passed, he imagined them coming to life, pummeling him with apples, oranges, watermelons and squash, his overactive imagination playing tricks on him as he tried to stay far ahead of the mob that was hounding after him. He quickly left the square, his legs pumping as hard as they could, and headed down the dark alley straight to the unlocked door of the *Ledoux Chocolaterie* where Armand and Tumelo secretly awaited his arrival.

Quickly closing the door behind him, the boy ducked under a display table in the dark shop while Pignoli and Fleur stirred anxiously in his top pocket before poking out their tiny heads.

"Ahh, thank goodness we are finally inside the *chocolaterie*," said Pignoli, breathing a sigh of relief while yawning and stretching his arms. "Did we give the bloodhounds the slip?"

"I believe so," Hammett whispered, his chest heaving up and down as he tried to catch his breath. "There does not seem to be anyone else out there." Of course, he would keep a cautious eye on the large shop window overlooking the alley just the same.

"This is indeed a pretty little *chocolaterie*," Fleur commented while looking around the dark shop, for she could see it perfectly without the lights on, "much prettier than the alley behind it."

Slowly getting back on his feet, Hammett had to agree, admiring his favorite surroundings once again as he switched on the lights.

"Is it not the most enchanting little place you have ever seen?" he asked. "And look at how pretty the chocolates are too."

"Excuse me," said Pignoli, tapping lightly on the boy's chest, "would you be so kind as to obtain a lovely *bonbon* for Fleur and me?" The tiny mouse licked his lips.

"I would be most happy to get you a *bonbon*," said Hammett, looking for the prettiest one in the shop.

In the meantime, Armand and Tumelo were both behind the partition, spying on the young intruder. "Do you see that, my dear?" Armand whispered to his wife. "Do you believe me now when I tell you that this boy talks into his top pocket, just as though there were someone in there?"

"I would never have believed it if I had not heard it with my own ears," acknowledged Tumelo. She looked at her husband earnestly. "I believe the time has come, dear husband, for you to confront your chocolate thief."

Even with his wife's encouragement, Armand hesitated at first as though he regretted having to interrupt the boy's enjoyment. But after gulping down a large breath of air, he quickly came to his senses. Stepping out from behind the partition, followed closely by Tumelo, he was now ready to confront the boy. Yes...the time had finally come.

"Who are you, boy?" Armand asked gently so as not to scare away his young intruder. Hammett froze to his spot, unsure of how to respond, but once he got over the initial shock of having been caught, he figured that it was best to be honest.

"My name is Hammett, kind sir, and I come to you from the Ouble' Orphanage. I mean no harm by being here. As a matter of fact, I like your *chocolaterie* very much, and would give anything to work in such a place." Tumelo was instantly touched, putting her hand to her heart.

The orphan boy trembled slightly as he told the kindly old couple his entire story—how he only wanted to make his Trista happy by giving her chocolate; how he had to sneak past the sleeping nursemaid at the orphanage after nightfall to make the trip into the village by the light of a lantern he had taken from the potter's shed; and how he made a mess of the *chocolaterie* on his first visit because he felt rushed and nervous, but how after that he grew to admire and appreciate the lovely little shop, a place where he would one day like to work. Armand and Tumelo exchanged glances as the boy stood there and bit his lip, still trembling.

"You poor child," said Tumelo, telling Hammett to sit down. "Who is this Trista, my dear boy? She must be someone awfully special for you to go through all that trouble just to get her some chocolate."

Hammett blushed…noticeably. "She is a friend of mine at the orphanage," he said, "a special friend."

"Oh, I see," said the kindly old woman with a gentle and understanding smile. Armand suddenly jumped into the conversation.

"How did you pull it off, Hammett?" he asked. "How did you ever leave the orphanage without getting caught? And another thing," he started immediately, not giving the boy a chance to answer his first question, "how did you find your way into the village, and then to our *chocolaterie*, in the dark of night with only a small lantern to light your way?"

At that point, Pignoli stirred in the boy's top pocket. "Tell him," gloated the tiny mouse, poking a finger at the boy right through his shirt.

"Quiet," whispered Hammett while placing a gentle hand to his chest, not wanting Armand and Tumelo to see his squirming pocket. Besides, he would never put it past Pignoli to poke his head out and simply introduce himself. *Mon deau*!

"And that is another thing," said the *chocolatier*, raising his voice and shaking a finger at Hammett, "you are always talking into your top pocket! What do you have in there?"

"Dear sir, I would *like* to answer all of your questions, but I fear that your *chocolaterie* will soon be overrun by a mob of people sent by Signora Nonmaltobello to hunt me down," said the boy.

"Ah, yes…the matron," Armand said with a smirk. "I have made her acquaintance…quite an unpleasant woman. Nevertheless, I would still like the answers to my…"

Suddenly, the old gentleman was rudely interrupted when the door to his *chocolaterie* flew open, and a group of Signora Nonmaltobello's unsavory searchers pushed their way into the shop.

"There he is!" they shouted. "Grab him!"

"You will do no such thing!" Armand exclaimed, standing in front of Hammett while Tumelo quickly followed suit, linking her arm into that of her husband's. "The boy is here under the protection of my wife and I, so you will kindly leave our *chocolaterie* at once!"

"We have strict orders from Signora Nonmaltobello, dear sir, to bring the boy back to her," said one of the nursemaids, out of breath

80

but spoiling for the capture of the elusive orphan.

"You will give your matron this message from me," ordered Armand, "that the boy will remain with us permanently, and that I will drive out to the orphanage tomorrow to make the formal and binding arrangements."

"But...but...I cannot just permit you to *keep* the boy here tonight," said the exasperated nursemaid, stumbling over her words.

"You can, and you will!" the *chocolatier* shouted, herding the stunned group toward the door. Hammett stood perfectly still, astonished by the unexpected announcement of Armand Ledoux. Two joyful mice poked their heads out of the boy's top pocket and looked around.

"Now, *this* is what I call an adventure with a happy ending," said a smiling Pignoli.

"One more thing, Monsieur Ledoux," the exasperated nursemaid managed to get out. "Where is the orphan girl?"

"I do not know *what* you are talking about," Armand said emphatically. "There *is* no orphan girl here. Ask him!" he said, gesturing toward Hammett.

"I came here alone," confirmed the boy, "and that is the truth."

With that, Armand pushed the disagreeable mob out of the *chocolaterie* and slammed the door shut, freeing Hammett and his two tiny friends of Signora Nonmaltobello and the Ouble' Orphanage...forever.

When the group of nursemaids and groundskeepers returned to the orphanage, they headed straight for Trista's room, afraid to report directly to Signora Nonmaltobello, just yet. Quietly opening the door and peeking in while the rest remained out in the hallway, the nursemaid who had been so outspoken at the *chocolaterie* found the orphan girl indeed...sound asleep in her bed.

"She is here!" she whispered, silently backing out of Trista's room on tiptoe before closing the door. "What are we ever going to tell Signora Nonmaltobello? The girl appears to be innocent of any wrongdoing, and we were foiled from bringing the boy back with us...even though he was right within our grasp! The matron is not going to like this!"

Looking at each other with frightened eyes before scattering quickly, the nursemaids ran to their bedrooms and locked their doors behind them, while the groundskeepers shut themselves up in the potter's shed. None of them looked forward to the inevitable wrath of the foul matron who was sure to make a scene. Hopefully, the night would pass peacefully for everyone, leaving it up to Armand Ledoux to deal with Signora Nonmaltobello the next morning.

As for Trista, unaware of what had happened in the village, she continued to dream innocently...of chocolate.

Chapter 13

What Goes Up Must Come Down

Armand got up bright and early the next day, anxious to go back to the Ouble' Orphanage and take legal charge of Hammett. "I must have my small trunk of magic tricks," insisted the orphan boy, "but that is not my only concern. What will become of my Trista?"

"You will be allowed to visit her often," the *chocolatier* assured him.

"And bring her chocolate too," said Tumelo who had also gotten up early to see them off. She placed a gentle hand on the boy's arm, for she could tell that he was nervous about leaving the orphan girl behind.

"But suppose the matron is cruel to Trista? I will no longer be there to protect her," Hammett lamented. Tumelo looked at her husband sadly, for her memory was long and she recalled just how harsh the matron was, all those years ago, when she and Armand were children at the Ouble' Orphanage. Her heart broke for the boy, but there was nothing more she could say...not just yet.

Upon arriving at the orphanage later that morning, Armand put his arm around Hammett's shoulders as they walked up the steps together. Although the boy was thrilled about leaving the orphanage as a *chocolatier's* apprentice, he obviously dreaded having to see Signora Nonmaltobello for fear that something would go...terribly wrong.

"Do not worry," said Armand. "I will do all of the talking."

"But...she is so *foul*," said Hammett.

"Indeed," chuckled the *chocolatier*. "Most foul."

"Most foul is right!" echoed Pignoli as he and Fleur poked their heads out of the boy's top pocket.

"Mind your manners," Hammett whispered to Pignoli. "I am anxious enough!"

"I guess I will have to get used to you talking into your top pocket," Armand laughed, "*and* the two little friends to whom you always talk!" he added jovially, patting Pignoli and Fleur on their tiny heads before entering the orphanage with a nervous Hammett in tow.

Signora Nonmaltobello was there to greet them at the door, her mood most foul indeed.

"So, you have finally decided to bring the boy back to me," the matron seethed through clenched teeth. "He will be severely punished for leaving the orphanage."

"There is no need to punish the boy," Armand said quickly, putting a hand up. "He has done nothing wrong."

"Are you telling me that he is not your chocolate thief?" asked Signora Nonmaltobello abruptly. "I just assumed..."

"You assume incorrectly, dear woman," Armand countered, not wanting to give the matron the satisfaction of being correct...even though she was. "The chocolate thief was caught days ago."

"No matter, Monsieur Ledoux," the matron snapped, "for I saw the boy leave the orphanage with a friend. And I do not know how she managed it," she continued in a menacing tone, now turning her attention away from the *chocolatier* to Hammett, "but the orphan girl who left with you was, somehow, able to return...undetected. She will also be punished for her sneakiness."

"I have no idea what you are talking about, dear Matron," said the boy, "for I left the orphanage alone."

"And it is he alone who accompanies me here this morning," Armand confirmed in a reassuring voice, expecting the matron to be reasonable.

"No child runs away from the Ouble' Orphanage under the watch of Signora Nonmaltobello!" she shouted, banging her fist on a table. "I know what I saw and both orphans will pay for what they did! They will go to bed without supper for a month, wash every floor and window in the building, and finally...I will take a paddle to them both until they can no longer sit down!" The matron was absolutely hysterical, and Armand realized that he could no longer expect her to be reasonable.

"You shall do no such thing," Armand shot back in response to Signora Nonmaltobello's tirade, "for the boy will not spend another night under this roof! I am here to adopt him and make him my apprentice, and I demand that you present me with the necessary papers at once!" he shouted, this time he being the one to bang his fist on the same table. Hammett could hardly breathe but could crack a slight smile, for the *chocolatier* had finally put the foul matron in her place.

Although Signora Nonmaltobello had met her match in Armand Ledoux, she could not resist one last opportunity to dig at Hammett's heart, for it was she who must always have the last, nasty word. "I will get the necessary papers from my office immediately," she growled at Armand with a raised brow, turning on her heels to leave. But as she came upon the boy on her way out, she suddenly stopped and made an ominous remark in her most foul tone: "I am not surprised that you would leave your friend here to suffer the consequences alone, and believe me...she *will* suffer." The matron then smiled with deliberate cruelty.

Before the boy could respond, he and Armand suddenly found Tumelo standing there, having walked through the front door of the Ouble' Orphanage just in time to hear the matron's savage remark. They found the dear old woman to be determined, for her memory was long indeed, and her best memory of the orphanage was when she and Armand walked out of there...together.

"She will do no such thing," Tumelo stated triumphantly, countering the matron's cold-blooded remark, thus denying her the last word.

"Tumelo!" Armand exclaimed with delighted surprise, most happy to see his dear wife. "What are you doing here?"

"I have been thinking, ever since you and Hammett left the shop this morning to come here, that it would be wrong to leave the girl behind. She must come home with us as well, dear husband, for it is obvious that the boy cares for her. We shall train them both, and when the time is right, they will take over the *Ledoux Chocolaterie.*"

"But, Tumelo," Armand countered, "are you absolutely sure that you want to adopt *two* apprentices?"

"Think back, my dear," began the kindly old woman, placing a gentle hand on her husband's shoulder. "Would you have left the Ouble' Orphanage without *me*?" With that said, the *chocolatier* needed to think no further on the subject.

"You will bring me the necessary papers for *both* children!" he immediately ordered Signora Nonmaltobello, looking her straight in the eye.

"This is highly irregular," spat the matron in her most foul tone of voice. "I do not know if I can grant your request." Armand knew right away that she was merely being willful and stubborn, for the Ouble' Orphanage was *always* looking, even when he and Tumelo lived there as children, to discharge as many orphans as possible to whomever would take them, thus cutting down on the number of mouths to feed. As a matter of fact, only five years ago it became well known throughout the village that an old farmer and his wife had adopted five children at once! Signora Nonmaltobello had simply failed to realize that the old *chocolatier* had a long memory too.

"You *can* and you *will*!" he bellowed at the matron, once again banging his fist on the table. To Armand's surprise, she this time jumped at his command, too startled by his booming voice to refuse him. Finally, the difficult, foul, and nasty Signora Nonmaltobello... had surrendered.

After the matron had left the room to retrieve the necessary papers, Pignoli scrambled out of Hammett's top pocket and down to the floor without being noticed, for the boy was wholly captivated by the events unfolding in front of him. The tiny white mouse was determined to, somehow, make known his dislike for the foul, screeching woman who had brought him here in a carpetbag. Perhaps a simple bite on the ankle would do, or a climb up her long skirt. He stood in a corner and thought about it long and hard as Fleur waved at him with a small handkerchief from her place in the boy's pocket as though he were going off...to war.

While Signora Nonmaltobello was still in her office looking for those papers, Armand ordered a nursemaid, who happened to be standing there with her mouth wide open, to escort Hammett to his room to retrieve his things, especially the small trunk of magic tricks.

"You will then gather the girl and all of *her* things," the *chocolatier*, now feeling emboldened, commanded the nursemaid, "bringing *both* children back to me, ready to leave this place."

"Yes, Monsieur," said the demure nursemaid, curtsying ever so slightly in front of Armand.

Tumelo was so proud of her husband for not allowing Signora Nonmaltobello to give him orders or treat him cruelly the way their own matron had done...all those years ago. And how simply lovely it would be to have not only one, but two young people in whom they could entrust their beloved Ledoux Chocolaterie. She placed a gentle hand on his arm and smiled, for everything was as it should be. By a simple stroke of the pen, Hammett and Trista would soon have a whole new life.

The nursemaid came back quickly with the two orphans, for neither of them had much in the way of personal belongings other than a few articles of clothing and, of course, the small trunk of magic tricks. Trista never expected such a wonderful surprise. Not only would she, too, be leaving the Ouble' Orphanage as an apprentice to Armand and Tumelo Ledoux, but she would still see Hammett every day. The fact that she would be surrounded by chocolate for the rest of her life had hardly sunk in. She smiled from ear to ear, and would remember this day...forever.

Just as they began to wonder what was keeping Signora Nonmaltobello, the rattled matron came back with a pile of papers to be signed by both Armand and Tumelo. The kindly old couple sat at a small table and signed each paper presented to them, officially making Hammett and Trista their adopted apprentices. The two children watched proudly and when the dear old couple stood up, the former orphans hugged their benefactors with tender affection. It was at that very moment when Hammett realized that Pignoli was no longer in his pocket. Now what?

It was quite obvious to everyone in the room that Signora Nonmaltobello now wanted to make a hasty exit without saying goodbye to anyone, not even the children. She turned to quickly walk away, but had to stop and wait, for a cook from the kitchen was headed toward the dining room with a large bowl of gruel and had walked right in front of the humiliated matron, blocking her way. Suddenly, the cook screamed, throwing the bowl high up in the air. It seemed that a tiny white mouse had skittle-skattled up her skirt and tickled her elbow.

"Souris! Souris!" the cook screamed, running from the room in fright, waving her arms frantically above her head.

Hammett knew instantly that it was Pignoli who had scared the cook, for not only was he missing, but it was also the very thing that the rascally little mouse would do. The boy's eyes frantically searched the floor for his friend as an uproar of laughter erupted throughout the room, the nursemaid laughing the hardest. It seemed that the large bowl of gruel had come back down exactly where the tiny white mouse had intended, having landed right on top of Signora Nonmaltobello's head. Flustered and dripping with the watery mixture, the foul matron stormed out of the room and out of the lives of Hammett and Trista...forever.

As good fortune would have it, when the bowl of gruel went up in the air, Pignoli was able to skittle-skattle back down the cook's skirt and onto the floor where artistic splats and curvy puddles of the boiled oatmeal soon surrounded him...much to his delight!

"There he is!" Fleur shouted, her dainty little head sticking out of Hammett's top pocket. The mouse was there indeed, sitting on the floor nearby, merrily licking up a large splat of gruel. The boy quickly scooped up his tiny friend and dropped him back into his pocket, certain of the role he had played in the messy fiasco.

"You did that on purpose," Hammett whispered to Pignoli with a smile.

"It would have been rude not to give Signora Nonmaltobello a *special* farewell," the mouse whispered back, still licking his lips.

"You are a naughty little boy," Hammett replied, winking at his friend. But before there could be any further conversation between Hammett and his top pocket, Armand and Tumelo Ledoux gathered their two newly adopted apprentices and whisked them away from the Ouble' Orphanage for good. And to Pignoli, that was the best adventure...of all!

Afterword

And so it went that the orphan boy who kept a small trunk of magic tricks and the orphan girl who loved chocolate were now the apprentices of Armand and Tumelo Ledoux, the kindly old couple who would teach them how to be *chocolatiers*... and so much more.

Hammett took his lessons from Armand quite seriously, quickly learning how to make, mold, dip, and decorate chocolates of all sorts in many fine and colorful ways. He also made the special creams that filled the *bonbons* in strict accordance with the scrumptious recipes handed down by Armand's great-grandfather, the very first Ledoux to open up a *chocolaterie* in the village of Le Clerc.

The boy apprentice was also shown how to glaze the fruits and make the marshmallows, his two least favorite jobs given the stickiness of their nature, as well as chop the nuts, color the sugars, and mix the fondant.

"You must learn how to clean up after yourself too," Armand insisted. "Every good *chocolatier* knows how to clean up after himself."

Added to this, Hammett learned how to wrap up each chocolate bar he made with decorated tissue paper ordered specially from Paris and tie it off with a pretty silk ribbon. If the delicate paper crinkled or ripped, or if the fine silk ribbon rested crookedly on top of the chocolate bar, then Armand would make him start all over again...and again...and again until he got it right. Finally, the boy waited on customers, swept the floor, kept the tables and counters sparkling clean, washed the windows inside and out...and learned how to make coffee every morning for Armand and himself.

So, it was no surprise that every night he would collapse onto the small cot in the dark corner behind the partition in the *chocolaterie*, his dreams having already come true while his head was filled with the sweet smell of chocolate.

As for Trista, she took her lessons quite seriously too, most of them from Tumelo. Even though she joined Hammett early every morning in the making, molding, dipping, and decorating of each fine chocolate, she also learned other important aspects of the business, such as shopping in the village square for the finest ingredients.

"The nuts must be plump and meaty," Tumelo would say, "while the fruits must be ripe...but not *too* ripe." Trista watched closely as the kindly old woman pinched and squeezed *everything* before buying it, each ingredient having to be just right. "Make sure, too, that the powdered sugar is sparkling white, for sometimes they try to sneak brown sugar into the mix which absolutely *ruins* the chocolate," Tumelo would insist. "And the butter must be as creamy as...chocolate mousse."

Trista's favorite part of going to market was when they finished their business and Tumelo would bring her to the lemonade stand. "It is now time for refreshment," she would say, "for buying all the right ingredients is no easy task." Tumelo would then pat her sweating forehead with a linen handkerchief before thirstily gulping down a glass of tart lemonade, while Trista slowly drank hers through a straw. The young girl never *had* lemonade at the orphanage and straws were, well...unheard of.

Tumelo also taught Trista how to order other ingredients and necessary supplies from Paris, such as the extraordinary cocoa powder that Armand liked to use in his chocolate, and the pretty tissue paper and silk ribbon needed to wrap the chocolate bars. Most importantly, she instructed her on how to handle all the bills and accounts related to the *chocolaterie* while, at the same time, giving her some sage advice.

"You must always spend your money wisely, pay your bills on time and, of course, be kind to *everyone* you meet," said the dear old woman. "If you follow these simple rules after Armand and I are gone, especially the last one, then you will be rich beyond your expectations."

Trista did not even want to *think* about the day when the beloved couple would no longer be there but the former orphan girl, who never had any possessions to speak of, was quite pleased with the thought of being rich beyond her expectations... and she said so to Tumelo.

"Oh, no, my dear," the old woman said gently. "You misunderstood my advice. It will be your *heart* that is rich, knowing that you spent your money wisely, paid your bills on time, and were kind to *everyone* you met...not your pocketbook. Always remember that material wealth is of little value when you have a rich heart."

It was no surprise that such a notion would come from the kindly old Tumelo, and Trista would remember it for the rest of her life. Her heart grew richer with each passing year...just by knowing her.

As for Pignoli and Fleur, they were on an adventure of which most mice could only dream! To live in a *chocolaterie* was not at all common for a mouse living in the village of Le Clerc, and actually unheard of in well-known mouse circles. The alleyway behind the *chocolaterie*, once home to Fleur, was the place more frequently inhabited by little squeakers, given its overflowing garbage cans, although a smart Le Clercan mouse would never overlook the carts of fruits, vegetables and other treats found in the village square. It was the spot where most clever mice gathered if they wanted a change from the alleys, for the cuisine was absolutely scrumptious.

Pignoli spent his days in a comfortable nest of soft rags and old socks, set in a far-off corner of the *chocolaterie* where no one could see him. Every once in a while, he would skittle-skattle around the floor to exercise or relieve his boredom, but this was strictly forbidden by Armand if there was a customer in the shop.

Pignoli liked to lick up the occasional chocolate crumbs or gather any soft pieces of silk ribbon that he could find to place in his nest. He ate well, especially in the afternoon, his favorite meal consisting of cheese, beef, and mashed potatoes...not to mention, of course, chocolate. Fleur joined him for every meal and the two of them would scurry and play every evening after the shop had closed.

At bedtime, Pignoli would curl up in his favorite familiar place, Hammett's top pocket, and dream sweet dreams of chocolate and adventure, while Fleur preferred to sleep in Tumelo's sewing basket. The demure little mouse was quite fond of the sewing basket, sitting inside it or next to it whenever Tumelo allowed her to do so.

If the kindly old woman happened to be making a dress for Trista, or a shirt for Hammett, Fleur would most certainly be somewhere nearby, waiting for the tiny scraps to fall to the floor so that she could bring them to Pignoli for his nest. What fun that was!

Although Tumelo's sewing basket was her favorite resting place, Fleur especially loved it when the dear old woman would allow Trista to take her and Pignoli along to market. Of course, the two mice would have strict instructions to stay out of sight until they were given permission to poke their heads out and smell the vast array of market aromas but, nonetheless, it was always the greatest adventure of which *any* mouse would be envious. Being such good mice, for they were always obedient, would ensure that Trista gave them their much-anticipated bits of apple or, if they were *really* lucky, a lick of powdered sugar off her finger.

Not only had Pignoli and Fleur found each other, thanks to Hammett, but they also lived the best skittle-skattle life ever, far better than that of any other mouse in the village of Le Clerc, the kind of which well-bred mice could only fancy...in their dreams. Even Pignoli could not have imagined such a life of adventure and glory before he would go from the Arancia train station, to a dark carpetbag, to the Ouble' Orphanage, and finally to this wonderful place...the *Ledoux Chocolaterie*. A most fortunate mouse he was indeed!

The years passed and the time came when Armand and Tumelo Ledoux were ready to place their beloved *chocolaterie* in the capable hands of Hammett and Trista. No longer children, they were now fine *chocolatiers* who were well prepared to run the shop on their own. The two former apprentices proved their talents every day too, for the chocolates they made easily rivaled those created in Paris. The kindly old couple was content, for they had trained their apprentices well, and the chocolates for which they were so admired would still be enjoyed by the good people of Le Clerc and beyond...for years to come.

Hammett and Trista were proud of their work at the *Ledoux Chocolaterie*, for they took on their tasks each and every day with kind hearts, just as their dear benefactors had lovingly taught them. No longer inexperienced, their names would be forever known throughout the village as two of the finest *chocolatiers* since Armand and Tumelo. They were a devoted couple too, now married and the adoring parents of Baptiste and Louise, two children they had adopted from the Ouble' Orphanage. The *Ledoux Chocolaterie* would now live on...for generations.

And what became of Signora Nonmaltobello you might ask, the most foul matron to ever work at the Ouble' Orphanage? Alas! She was now putting her talents to better use as the person in charge of sweeping and garbage collection at the Arancia train station where new adventures were sure to begin!

Everything was as it should be...thanks to Pignoli and the Chocolate Thief.

Fin.

Hammett's Sloppy Fistfuls of Smashed Chocolates and Cream

Ingredients
- 12 ounces of whipped cream cheese
- 12 chocolate sandwich cookies (You can add 2 or 3 more if you like)
- Approximately 7.2 ounces of your favorite milk chocolate (16 small snack size bars or the smallest milk chocolate chips you can find)
- Small (bite size) paper baking cups (Do not worry—there is no baking!)
- Approximately 6 ounces of your favorite dark chocolate melting wafers

Preparation Time
Approximately 1 hour...if the other orphans leave me alone!

Directions
1. In a food processor blend your 12 chocolate sandwich cookies until they are pretty crumby. If you do not have a food processor, then place the cookies in a gallon-sized freezer bag and smash them until all the large pieces are gone. Then pour the chocolate crumbs into a bowl. I never let Signora Nonmaltobello hear me do this!

2. Fold in the 12 ounces of whipped cream cheese (either in the food processor or in the bowl) and blend well with the chocolate cookie crumbs. This will be a pretty thick mixture. It is at this time that Pignoli will try to stick his hands in the bowl!

3. Add the milk chocolate into the chocolate cookie crumb and whipped cream cheese mixture and blend. In the food processor, blend the chocolate well but do leave it a little chunky. If you are mixing everything in a bowl then either break up your milk chocolate bars into the smallest pieces you can, or simply substitute tiny milk chocolate chips and blend in well. This is the part that Trista likes best!

4. Now is a good time to set-up your small paper baking cups. I use a large baking sheet covered with parchment paper and

place approximately 30 small cups on it. Fleur usually helps me set up the cups!

5.   With a teaspoon, drop a generously sized dollop of well-blended chocolate cookie crumb, whipped cream cheese, and chocolate chunks mixture into each small paper-baking cup. Be prepared to get chocolate on your hands. This is when Pignoli tries to lick the chocolate off my fingers!

6.   Melt approximately 6 ounces of dark chocolate melting wafers in the microwave. I like to do it in a glass-measuring cup. Set the microwave to defrost and melt the chocolate wafers at 15-second intervals, stirring well each time until the chocolate is smooth. Tumelo taught me that!

7.   Drizzle the melted chocolate over the mixture in each paper-baking cup. Armand watches over my shoulder to make sure that I do not miss a single cup!

8.   Place the entire baking sheet in the refrigerator and allow the mixture to set overnight. Ignore impatient mice!

Bon Appetit!